SMOKIN'
HOT
FIREMEN

SMOKIN' HOT FIREMEN

EROTIC ROMANCE STORIES FOR WOMEN

EDITED BY
DELILAH DEVLIN

FOREWORD BY
JO DAVIS

CLEiS
PRESS

Published in the United States by Cleis Press, Inc.,
2246 Sixth Street, Berkeley, California 94710.

Printed in the United States.
Cover design: Scott Idleman/Blink
Cover photograph: Peter Dazeley/Getty Images
Text design: Frank Wiedemann

First Edition.
10 9 8 7 6 5 4 3 2 1

Trade paper ISBN: 978-1-57344-934-2
E-book ISBN: 978-1-57344-951-9

Contents

INTRODUCTION

Dear Reader,

When I was asked to tell you what I find so very special about firefighters and why I chose to write about them, I was thrilled. Firefighters rank number one on the list of my very favorite subjects, and I'm more than happy to reveal exactly why they never fail to get me all steamed up.

Firefighters command respect. Just mention firefighters or speak of one you happen to know, and you immediately have everyone's undivided attention. Better yet, let one enter the room and feel the shiver, watch folks stand up a little straighter, as the unspoken thread of respect winds around every single person present. Everyone wants to be near them, to hear what they have to say.

Firefighters are courageous. In the event of a disaster, firefighters represent our best hope when all seems lost. They are our real-life superheroes. They are fathers, mothers, sisters, brothers, husbands, or wives. They put their lives on the line for you and me without sparing a thought for their own. We cheer when they succeed and we mourn for those who don't go home. Firefighters are a slice of Americana, dynamic men and women who represent the heart of what makes our country so great. When everyone else is running away from danger, they run straight into it to save us. No matter the cost.

Firefighters are damned sexy. May or December, tall or short, fair or dark, these men make my blood boil in the best way possible. There's just something thrilling about seeing a fireman in his turnouts, sweaty and satisfied from accomplishing a job well done, or wearing his department T-shirt on the way to the gym, muscles on glorious display as he turns every head. Firemen are quite simply divine. They should come with their own "contents under pressure" warning label!

Is it any wonder I adore them? I'll shamelessly admit that I'd love to have a fireman of my very own to heat up my bed and warm my heart—to make me feel like I'm the most treasured gift in his universe. Barring that miracle? I'll simply live vicariously and read all about their brave, gorgeous selves, and I invite you to do the same.

So don your gear, make yourself comfy, and get your fire hose ready in case these guys get just a little too hot to handle— you're in for a five-alarm treat. Enjoy!

Jo Davis

National bestselling author of these series:
The Firefighters of Station Five
Sugarland Blue
Armed and Deadly

FOREWORD

I'm writing this little introduction in the middle of a scorching summer. With no rain for more than a month, trees are wilting, grass is burned to a crisp, and fire is an ever-present worry. Every time I click the TV remote, images of fires sweeping across the Western states drive home the lurking danger.

One spark can end a life, destroy a home.

Images of firefighters dressed in their bulky gear bombard me. They dig deep trenches and cut timber in forests, preparing breaks to halt fires from sweeping through rural communities. Their chutes billow around them as they fall through the air only to land in places most sane folks would flee. They speed through city streets, jumping from their big trucks, carrying hoses and axes, to enter buildings engulfed in flames, risking their lives to save ours.

Heroes don't just fight in far-flung deserts; they live in our neighborhoods and fight the battles we aren't prepared to wage.

Just the mention of the word "firefighter" inspires a jumble of sexy images: a soot-covered face; sweat dripping from hard, chiseled muscles; the sexy snap of suspenders—yes, only a fireman can make suspenders sexy!

Then imagine the romantic possibilities of being held against that massively muscled chest by a man whose mission is to save lives—a physically powerful man in his prime whose instincts are honed to rush into danger...

Melting yet? You will be.

Delilah Devlin

SMOKING STILETTOS

Rachel Firasek

The metal door leading into the garage slammed against the concrete, startling me from my tears. "Ooh, he's really pissed."

"Climb in back and stay down." Derek, my husband's best friend and my almost-always savior, opened the driver's-side door and lunged to the ground.

He didn't bother shutting it behind him. One of the fire trucks was still drying out front after being hosed down, so I had an opportunity to watch the two men.

"Hey, Matt. What's up?"

I peeked over the back window sill from the rear seat and winced at the red ring climbing up my husband's throat. Soon he'd resemble a tomato. Not good for a man on the cusp of high blood pressure at thirty-five. Even if he did irritate the hell out of me, I wanted him to have plenty more years on Earth.

Matt flexed his shoulders. "Don't. Where is she?"

Derek held both hands up, palms cupped like he might need to catch hold of Matt when he came at me. And he would. Oh, not in a violent way—no, not my honey. But he would make me pay.

"What did she do now?"

Matt pulled his shaggy hair back, revealing a thin bleeding cut above his temple. "She threw a fucking designer stiletto at me. Cut the shit out of me. I'll probably have to have Doc look at it before I go on duty."

Derek's chuckle echoed in the empty garage. "Damn. What did you do?"

Matt shrugged, and a dimple formed beneath the right corner of his lip. He hated that dimple, but I thought it was the cutest thing ever.

"Nothing."

"Matt?"

"What?" Matt blew out a deep breath. "So I told her about the Twenty-Fifth Street fire. She overreacted and kicked her foot at me. I don't think either of us expected her shoe to fly off, but it did." He snorted. "While I'm on the floor, holding my eye, she darts out the damn door."

That was only half of our problem. I had overreacted, but he also knew that every time he came home and told me those horrible stories about burning bodies and devastating destruction, I saw him taking the place of the people he saved. When he was on the night shift, I woke up in cold sweats, worrying. I missed appointments—and as an assistant at one of the most prestigious law firms in Manhattan, I couldn't afford the distraction. I found myself skipping dinner, worrying over *that* call.

So when he came home to tell me yet another of those stories like running into an inferno was just another day at the office, I lost it. He couldn't really blame me for that.

Derek hung his head, his shoulders shaking with a deep rumble of laughter. "That's why she only had one shoe!"

"I knew she'd run to you."

My friend and savior had ratted me out. The bastard. "Derek, you are so dead to me."

Both men glanced toward the truck. Shit! I scooted across the backseat, flipped the handle, and half-slid, half-rolled to the ground below.

Derek's voice rose over the fire truck I'd used as my hideout. "Sorry, sweet angel, you did this all on your own."

The metal door leading to safety slammed shut and someone flipped the lock. Damn, I hated not being able to see.

"You can come out now, Red." Booted feet carried the words to the right, toward the cab of the truck. "There's nowhere to run and no one here to save you."

I reached down and pulled my remaining stiletto from my foot. Yes, I still wore it. The cabbie who had driven me to the station hadn't believed it either. I clutched that polka-dotted fave in my fingers and began to climb. The cold metal step carried me up to the deck with all the lines. I placed my toes on a hose coupling and pushed up, climbing the side of the truck as if my very life depended on it.

Matt veered around the corner of the truck and shouted, "Get your ass down here before you fall."

Yeah, not really the love I needed to coax me back down. I tossed my remaining shoe in his direction and kicked a leg over the top railing that kept the hoses in place above the tank. A black tarp draped across them kept me from slipping in the grooves. "You stay back and cool off, Mathew."

He placed his hands on his hips. "What now? Where you going to go?"

I glanced around. Damn, he'd cornered me after all. "Please," I began. He twisted his lips in that way he had when he didn't believe my pleading. "I mean it, baby. I'm sorry."

"Oh, you are not getting off that easy." He stepped up on the cab, wedging his boot against the back of the truck, and lunged up.

Christ, he could climb this thing much better than me. I shrieked and scrambled across the tarp. My knees screamed at me as the stretched fabric scraped them raw. "Ow."

A warm hand caught my ankle before I could climb over the other side. "Nuh-uh. Gotcha." He tugged and flipped me to my back in one smooth move.

My chest heaved, precious air wheezed down my throat, and a huge body pressed down on my poor, deprived lungs. "Oomph."

"Yeah, I should give you worse than that, brat." He stroked my hair away from my face and used his elbows, tucked close to my ears, to lift his weight away. "Calmed down now?"

I nodded, but frantically searched the area for a weapon. He'd never get me to really admit defeat. And have no doubt, that's what this game was about. I bucked my hips against him. "You can get up now."

"Nah, I like where I'm lying just fine." He wedged a knee between my thighs and settled between. "Better."

Better for him. Sure. I already felt just how much better he liked it against my stomach.

If I gave in to him now, he'd continue being the hero and taking chances with a life I considered mine—*his*. "Look. We. Need. To. Talk," I said.

"Nope. Tried that, and I'm bleeding for it. Now we do it my way."

He dropped his head. His green eyes flared a half-second before his lips landed on mine. In a way only two people who knew each other could, we came together with an intensity that startled me. Heat flooded south and mewling whimpered from my throat. Damn traitorous hormones. A large hand trailed down my neck, lower, to the first button on my blouse.

I reached up and caught his knuckles. "We can't."

"Why?"

"The guys in the kitchen. The fact that this is your job. I can keep going if you'd like."

That dimple peeked below his lip. "I don't mind."

He scooted down, releasing buttons as he went. The zipper on my skirt scratched loudly in the silent garage. "Matt."

He spread kisses above my navel. "Shhh...you owe me."

Two tugs and my skirt wrapped around one of my ankles. I sat up.

He caught my shoulder, forcing my back down, flattening me to the tarp. "Nope. You're going to pay. I think your sweet honey will do."

Oh, no. When he got like this, nothing would stop him. I fisted my hands at my sides and promised myself he wouldn't know how much his attitude turned me on.

He caught my thong in his hand and, with one rip, freed it from my body. So fucking sexy.

"Red, I think you've been bad. You hurt me. But I'm not going to hurt you. No. I'm going to remind you why you get so pissed. I'm going to show this body why you cry when I take chances."

His words hurt me deeper than he knew. I did cry, but far harder than I would ever actually share with him. Half of my tears fell out of guilt for wishing him home, and the other half for the fear he wouldn't ever make it back.

He dipped his head and bit my stomach just above my waxed mound. The sharp bite tugged at me, pushing away the thoughts cluttering my brain. The edges of those pearly whites slid down over my clit to catch onto the side of my labia.

"Spread for me."

My legs reacted to his command as if he'd spoken to them instead of me. He wedged them further apart with his shoulders and lowered his mouth to my pussy.

I felt the first shudder when he flicked his tongue against me. He added the soft abrasion of the stubble on his chin, and I shook.

"Pull up your knees."

Again, I did it without any back talk. I even helped out by grabbing my thighs and holding them apart for him. We both knew I wanted this as bad as he did.

He blew cool air against the damp trickle running down my crack, but didn't give me what I wanted. Needed. "Please."

"You like it?"

I nodded.

"You going to be a good little wife and keep your shoes on your feet?"

"Yes. Now. Please."

He bent forward, spread me with his large fingers, and attacked me with his tongue. The way I loved it. A finger joined in, and then two. When he thrust in three, I went over the edge, screaming his name and several other words we'd try to decipher later.

I sat up, caught his ears, and tugged his face up toward me. His lips found mine, and I mewled again at the taste of me on them. He fumbled with his zipper and I worked a hand beneath his T-shirt. "Hurry."

It took a moment before either of us heard the siren. Doors slammed, men shouted commands, and Matt raised his zipper. "Sorry, baby. We'll finish this later."

"What?"

"It's showtime. Get dressed."

Oh my God. We'd almost—no, we *had*—just had sex, sans penetration, on the bed of a fire truck in his freaking station.

He helped me slip on my blouse and wiggled my skirt up my thighs while I lifted my behind off the covered hoses.

Derek's laughter drifted up. "Should have known you two would be at it like animals by now."

Once I was dressed, Matt lowered me over the side into Derek's arms. "Take care of my girl for me. I'll gear up."

Really? After that, he'd just go to work? "Matt, what? You're not due to work for hours."

He shrugged. "But I'm here. Why not help out?"

Derek pushed me forward with a gentle shove and whispered in my ear. "If you zip it and get in the truck, I'm sure we'll be halfway there before he notices."

I twisted around. "Really? I can go?"

He raised a finger to his lips and opened the back door for me. "In."

The fire blazed through a three-story apartment building, lighting up the darkened neighborhood. "Oh, boy."

Derek tugged on one of my red curls. "Look. You keep your sweet ass in this truck. Matt will kill me if something happens to you."

I nodded, having a hard time taking my eyes away from the fire. "Okay."

Matt followed in the second truck, and all of the men abandoned the safety of the cab to roll out gear and head toward the flaming beast attacking those innocent people's homes. Police officers and other rescue professionals gathered the fleeing residents and ushered them to waiting ambulances.

With all the commotion, I couldn't wait. I hopped out of the truck and stopped at the curb. Matt's shock of dark brown hair disappeared beneath a helmet moments before he rushed inside the burning building.

My heart sped up and I sat down on the concrete lining the yard. The screams and cries of people watching their memories, hopes, and dreams crumble into ash filled the neighborhood.

A small child sat down beside me. I couldn't tell if it was a boy or a girl. Soot covered the child from head to toe.

"Hello." I reached out and wiped at the dirt covering the face. "Are you okay?"

"My mom's in there." Girl. She pointed toward a nearby ambulance. "She's burned."

I stroked her back. "I'm so sorry. I'm sure she'll be just fine."

The child laid her head on my lap and shook in bone-jarring shudders. I waved at a passing helper carrying a stack of blankets and draped one around the girl's thin shoulders. We waited together, watching the firefighters run in and out of the building, dragging bodies out on each pass.

Hours flew by in a busy stream of people. They took the child's mother away, but no one else had claimed the girl. I stayed, hoping I'd catch a police officer who could put her with a caseworker until her family could claim her. Surely someone would come soon.

A helmet cracked against the street seconds before a big yellow leg dropped down next to mine. "Who's your friend?" Matt's healthy, sparkling eyes watched me with weary creases at the corners.

"I don't know. I covered her up and she went to sleep." I stroked her hair. "They took her mom to the hospital a few hours ago."

Matt pulled off his gloves and rubbed a dirt-smudged hand against my neck. "You're freezing. How long did it take before you got out of the truck?"

"Not long." The last few snaps and crackles from the fire kept me from really sighing in relief. We all knew the blaze wasn't contained until all the hot spots had been doused. "Matt...all these people..."

"I know."

"I didn't know."

He rubbed at the tense muscles lining my shoulders.

"I'm so sorry."

He nuzzled his chin into my hair and placed a kiss against my head. "Shhh."

"No, I need to say it. All these years, I thought...I thought you did this for some crazy adrenaline rush, but seeing it up close...I...I'm so proud of you. What you're doing here is important. They need you."

He grinned, dimple flashing. "I know. But, Red, so do you. And I promise, I'm coming home to you every night or morning—depending on my shift. But it's always to you. You got me?"

I did. I so got him.

"Come on, let's get this little one with the right people and go home." He tugged my chin up and planted a sooty kiss across my cheek. "I've got plans for you and those stilettos."

SAVING CHARLOTTE

Sabrina York

M ark Conner fought his way through the smoke and flames to the third floor of the apartment building. A skitter of concern writhed in his gut. This fire was moving fast. Despite the nearly fifty pounds of equipment, he picked up the pace and motioned to Izzy to do the same.

According to the wailing mother on the street outside, there was a child still trapped up here.

Two doors flanked the top-floor landing. Without discussion—they hardly needed it anymore—Izzy turned right and Mark turned left. In tandem, they kicked in doors.

Mark angled his flashlight and scanned the smoky living room. Nothing. Smoke roiled around him; sweat prickled his brow. There wasn't much time.

Then he heard a faint cry. He shouldered his way down the hall and into the bedroom...and froze.

A second was far too long to stare. Lives could be lost in a second. But the sight that greeted him nearly brought him to his knees. A sudden, inappropriate lust snarled through him. He forced it to the back of his mind. For later.

He'd expected a small child, coiled in a corner.

Not an exquisite angel bound to a bed.

And she was exquisite. Her skin was milky white and shimmered in the caress of his flashlight beam. She writhed and cried out and fought at the bonds holding her down. Her lush hair was a dark cloud against the pillow. And her face...it took his breath away.

Tears scored her cheeks. Panic widened her eyes. "Help me," she said in a failing voice.

A loud pop brought him back to the moment. Yes, she was the most beautiful thing he'd ever seen—and he'd seen plenty of naked women tied to beds—but if he didn't get her out of here, she was going to die.

He rushed to her side and examined her bonds. He knew instinctively there was no time to untie her. Instead he reached for the cutting tool clipped to his belt and quickly slashed the ropes at her wrists and ankles. He wrapped her in a blanket and tossed her over his shoulder.

He met Izzy on the landing; his buddy held a small bundle in his arms. They nodded to each other and pounded hell for leather down the stairs. The building was weakening. Mark recognized the sounds, the feel of it. They had seconds to escape, if that.

They made it out—bursting through the door in a hail of fire and smoke—but only just. As they emerged out onto the street, the building collapsed behind them. A loud cry went up among the firefighters and they all snapped into action, training their hoses on the structure. The building was a lost cause, but they could save the neighboring homes.

Mark ignored the cacophony. He carried his precious burden across the barricaded street to the paramedics. Luke was busy fitting an old woman with an oxygen mask, and Samuel was wrapping a burn.

Gently, Mark lowered the woman from his shoulder. He arranged her on a brick planter, careful to keep her nakedness covered.

He pulled off his helmet, mask, and hood and unstrapped his SCBA gear to wipe the sweat from his brow. "A-are you all right?" Something clogged his throat. Probably an unholy reaction to her ethereal beauty.

Hell and damnation. She'd nearly died. How could he think about fucking her? His cock was thinking about it. It was hard and heavy and tight.

She nodded. A lone tear tracked its way down her sooty cheek.

He forced himself to look away from her delicate, sculpted features, her hollowed cheeks, her wide, doe-like eyes and trembling lips. Instead, he directed his attention to her wrists and began undoing the knots. He bit back a curse. Whoever had tied her up was an idiot. For one thing, the rope was bound far too tight. Even if she hadn't been fighting for her life to get free, it would have cut into her skin. As it was, her wrists were raw, slick with blood.

"You should have this tended." He didn't mean to sound so gruff. It galled him to see a woman abused like this. He released her wrists and went to work on her ankles. It took a while, because the knots were an undisciplined mess.

Mark knew he was delaying the inevitable, avoiding the question he had to ask. He hated to embarrass her after all she'd been through, but duty was duty. Reluctantly, he met her gaze—it seared him. He cleared his throat. "Do I...would you like me to notify the police?"

Her eyes widened. Lips formed a silent *no*.

"You weren't tied up against your will?"

Heat prickled his nerve endings when she lowered her lashes and shook her head.

Not against her will. Holy hell.

Mark glanced over his shoulder. The building was now a smoking relic. "Was he in the apartment?" He kind of hoped she'd say yes.

She didn't. "No. He t-tied me up and left."

Mark froze. His nostrils flared as outrage cut through him. What kind of Dom tied up a woman and *left*? "He left you?"

"Yes." Her voice was soft, sweet. Smoky. She studied her tender wrists for a moment, then met his gaze. "He went to the bar for a drink with some friends. Said I was to 'think about it' while he was gone."

What an ass.

Of course, no one would expect their house to catch fire while they were out gallivanting with friends, but leaving your trusting sub tied to the posts, exposed and vulnerable and completely alone, was unconscionable.

"How long have you been with him?" He didn't know why he asked. He was only torturing himself. She belonged to someone else.

"A year." She swallowed. Mark watched her throat work. He knew a raging urge to taste it. Lick it. Suck on that soft, creamy flesh... "We'd never tried this before."

Oh hell.

A dismal curtain fell on his soul. He'd assumed, from her lowered gaze, her posture, her submissive mien, that she was deep in the life, that she lived it, breathed it, craved it like he did. If this disastrous outing was her first taste of bondage, she would never try it again.

It was a pity, a damn shame he hadn't found her first.

He pitched his voice low, so no one else would hear. "For the record, a loving Dom never leaves his woman unprotected." He couldn't resist cupping her cheek, thumbing away the fresh tears that welled at his words. Couldn't resist a whispered "He doesn't deserve you."

She said nothing at that, but he could tell she'd heard him. Her expression took on a glow, a peace, and—dare he hope it—a tinge of relief.

Luke finished up with his patient and collected his bag to come over.

Mark knew it was time to release her. He didn't want to. He wanted to hold her forever. But she wasn't his.

Still, he couldn't resist leaning closer, capturing her gaze, and murmuring, "If you ever want to try this with someone who knows what he's doing, someone who will honor your desire, come to Station 12. Ask for Mark Conner."

Her lips parted in an astonished *O* and a shiver racked her frame. But she said nothing. With one last lingering look, he turned his back and walked away, knowing, in his heart of hearts, that he'd never see her again.

It was a shame. A damn, stinking shame.

She could have been the one.

She could have been everything.

It took Charlotte a month to dredge up the courage to take Mark Conner up on his offer. Breaking up with Bill had taken three minutes. An easy thing to do after what had happened. Her existing doubts about their relationship had only bolstered her resolve.

Besides, when Mark had stared into her eyes and issued his challenge, she'd known. She'd known she was just settling with Bill, that there could be so much more.

And she ached for more.

She'd always suspected she was a submissive. Had always craved a harsh hand on her ass. Ached to relinquish control to a strong partner. To be dominated completely—mind, body, and soul. But she'd never met a man with whom it felt right. She'd never met a man who made her feel like *that*. Not until Mark.

Still, it took her a month to get over the paralyzing fear. What if he was everything she'd ever dreamed? And what if he wasn't? What if she'd imagined the connection, the scorching passion between them? What if it had all been a construct of her mind, a reaction to the adrenaline surging in her veins?

What if he, like every other man she'd ever met, was a disappointment?

After weeks of driving herself crazy, she finally decided it was better to know than to wonder. And she made her way to Station 12.

The big garage door was open as she approached the firehouse. The trucks were out and parked in the driveway. A large, muscled man in tight jeans and a clingy blue T-shirt was in the process of coiling a hose on the floor of the bay. He looked up and broke into a smile.

"Well, hello there."

Charlotte flushed a little beneath the heat of his gaze. Yes, he was a gorgeous man. But he wasn't the man she wanted. "I'm looking for Mark Conner."

The cute fireman put out a lip. "Damn. Hey, Izzy, where's Conner?" he bellowed.

Another fellow leapt from one of the trucks. Charlotte recognized him from the night of the fire. Clearly, he recognized her too.

His brow arched. "You're here for Mark?" He blew out a whistle. "I think he's in the gym. Come on. I'll show you."

Charlotte followed Izzy to the back of the station. She tried to calm the butterflies in her stomach. Anticipation and dread warred within her. Would he be all she remembered? Could he?

Izzy paused at a door and, with a quick glance in her direction, pushed through.

She followed. The clang of weights, the smell of sweat assailed her. It was a small room, packed with workout equipment—treadmills, steppers, resistance machines, and barbells. It was also packed with half-naked men. The panoply of rippling muscle made her knees weak.

When they caught sight of her, they all froze, and silence blanketed the room—but for the growling snarl of one man hefting a heavy load.

Mark.

Charlotte's gaze found him and all the other preening men faded into the background. She stared at his chest, broad and straining, slick with sweat. The bulging muscles of his biceps quivered as he held the weight high; his neck bunched. The cut, ribbed surface of his abs tightened. His thighs—grounding him, steadying him—were like tree trunks.

Breath escaped her. A dizzying hum echoed in her head. Heavens. He was a titan.

He lowered the bar back into its holder with a grunt. He looked up. And froze.

They stared at each other for a long moment. His Adam's apple bobbed. Incredulity crossed his features, followed by a dark wash of hunger. At least she hoped it was hunger.

He stepped forward, grabbing his shirt. But he didn't put it on. He just used it to mop up his sweat.

"Hey Conner. You have a visitor," Izzy said in a sing-song voice that broke the spell.

All the other firefighters returned to their workouts.

But Charlotte was barely aware of them. She was barely aware of anything. Anything but Mark.

He stepped closer, scrubbing at his neck with the damp shirt.

His scent surrounded her. The smell of sweaty man, of hard, clean work. Of power. It made her tremble. Almost on autopilot—she'd practiced this for days—she put out her hand. "Mark Conner?"

"Yes."

His palm slipped into hers and electricity sizzled and spat between them. He was so warm. So big. She wanted him. He didn't release her hand right away. His thumb skimmed over her skin in a soft caress.

"Ch-Charlotte Raskin. I...I wanted to thank you for saving my life." There wasn't much more she could say, not here, surrounded by an avid audience.

But Mark knew. He knew there was more between them. He'd started it. He took her elbow and led her out of the gym, down the hall, and into a spotless, airy kitchen. When Izzy followed them, Mark shut the door in his face.

Suddenly they were alone. Mark stared at her as though he'd never seen anything quite so fascinating. It made her uncomfortable, warm. Little prickles of awareness coursed over her skin. Though he had done nothing, said nothing lurid, she felt her body soften and warm.

Restlessly, she shifted from one foot to the other.

He blinked as though jostled from a deep reflection. "I didn't think I'd ever see you again," he said. His voice was deep, rough.

"I was nervous about coming."

He raked his fingers through his hair. "Understandable. How are you doing?"

"Better."

His gaze scorched her. "Did you lose the loser?"

She couldn't hide her smile. "Of course."

"And did you think about what I said?"

"Of course."

"And?" Perhaps it was her imagination, but she thought she saw a flicker of doubt cross his tight expression.

"And...yes. If the offer is still good."

He blew out a harsh breath. "Oh, it's good." He stepped closer, so close she was enrobed in his heat. He put his hands on her shoulders and tugged her against his bare chest.

She skated her palm over his tanned muscles; they rippled at her touch. He was warm and hard and slick.

He growled low in his throat and bent his head. "Good," he murmured as his lips teased her cheek, her lids, her chin. "Good." And then, when she could bear the soft sweet tantalizing caress no longer, he settled his mouth fully on hers.

His taste was exquisite, his essence excruciating. Heat consumed her, burned her. The sensation of this man, this big muscled man, possessing her mouth made her weak. Made her wet.

She responded, giving him back the energy, the heat, the passion he gave her. His hands rose, roved. His fingers found her nipples, aching and swollen. She winced at his caress. Agony speared her. She burned with hunger for more.

His kiss intensified. He traced the seam of her lips with his tongue.

She quivered, opened to him.

"Ah," he breathed into her mouth.

And then he entered her.

It was only a pale reflection of what she really wanted. Nothing more than a kiss. But Charlotte was beyond logic. Her mind, her body, her soul were fully engaged in this tangling.

She came. A tiny shudder. A soft moan. A mere shadow of what was to come.

He pulled back, gasping. A feral light limned his expression. "Come home with me," he rasped. "Now."

It was his first command of her.

She could hardly refuse.

His apartment wasn't far from the fire station. He didn't know why he kept it, because he spent most of his time at work, but now he was glad he had someplace private to take her.

He closed the door behind her. It was all he could do to take it slow. What he wanted, what he really wanted, was to bend her over the couch and fuck her, right here, right now. But he couldn't. He wanted this to be right, to be perfect for her.

God help him, he didn't want some mindless tryst. Not with *her*. She was special. Maybe even the one he'd always searched for. He wanted to keep her. He wanted her to stay. Hell, he just plain wanted. Desperately.

"Take off your panties."

She jumped a little at the harsh tone of his voice, and he winced. He hadn't meant to be so abrupt. But then a light, that delicious, delightful light, gleamed in her eye. He knew she liked it.

She reached up beneath her skirt and slipped them off. She held them awkwardly, clutched in her fist. Her gaze dropped.

"Keep your eyes on me, Charlotte," he instructed. "Always on me."

With something akin to relief, she obeyed.

"Now put your panties on the table and sit. Lift up your skirt. I want your bare ass on the chair."

A flicker of panic crossed her face, but she did as he asked, flinching only slightly at the cool kiss of vinyl.

"Are you wet?"

She nodded.

"Tell me."

"Yes, I'm wet."

He *tsk*ed. Her idiot boyfriend had done no training whatso-ever. Mark wondered if the dipshit even knew the rules. "Call your Dom 'Master' or 'Sir.'"

"Yes, S-sir. I'm wet."

"Very good. Nice." He stepped behind her and, bless her, she tried to keep her eyes on him. "Do you really want this, Charlotte?" He settled his hands on her shoulders, slipped them lower to cup her breasts. They were full and soft and warm. Her nipples pressed on his palms. It was all he could do not to rub his thrumming cock against her back. He'd spent many nights, too many nights, thinking about this, aching for it.

"Yes, Sir."

"Have you thought about this like I have? Have you dreamed of this moment?"

She shuddered. "Yes, Sir."

He dipped his head and sucked on her earlobe. He let his mouth explore her fragrant neck and nest in the thick coils of her hair. "Did you touch yourself?"

"Y-yes."

His cock twitched at her error. He tightened his hold on her nipples, through the soft satin of her blouse, until she gasped. "Yes, *what?*"

"Yes, Sir." Her breath came out in low, trembling pants.

She was just as hungry as he was, just as lost to this. The knowledge seared him like a racing fire. "Lift your skirt."

Slowly, she drew up her hem. His heart thudded at the sight of her naked lips. He loved that she'd shaved for him.

"Open to me."

Ah. She knew, she just *knew*, what he wanted. She spread her legs and drew her swollen lips apart, exposing the thick bundle of nerves nestled there. It glistened.

"Are you wet for me, Charlotte?" His voice was a wraith, low and dark.

"Yes, Sir."

He roughly massaged her nipples.

She bit her lip to hold back a sob, but it escaped.

"Do you want me to touch it?"

"Oh, please." And then, after a moment, "Sir."

Mark moved around and dropped to his knees before her. He stared at her—open, welcoming, and wanting. He drew in her scent. It made him lightheaded. He could smell her arousal. Heat washed off her in waves. Her entire body quivered.

How he longed to taste her.

He wasn't a particularly patient man. Not at all a masochist. So he did. He dipped his head and drew his tongue along the length of her seam. She tasted like honey and cream. Delicious. When he dabbed her hard clit, she cried out. A dollop of glistening cream oozed from inside her.

Mark's heart stuttered at the sight. Smothering a groan, he yanked her closer and buried his face. He circled her swollen button with his tongue, glorying in her shivers, her cries, the feel of her nails scoring his scalp.

He sucked her in and nibbled, tightening his hold on her hips when she began to buck and plead.

"Hold still," he told her. But at the same time, he was determined to foment insurrection. He wanted her crazed with lust, clawing at his shoulders and writhing in his arms. He wanted her pleading for mercy and coming all over his tongue.

And he got what he wanted. She broke.

It began with small, stiff shudders and quickly grew to wild arching lunges. She wrapped her thighs around his head and thrust against him as he consumed her, sucking, licking, lapping, and flicking at that fat bundle of nerves.

When she tipped her hips, exposing the mouth of her cunt, he couldn't resist. He eased a thick finger into her scalding velvet channel. He pulled out—she protested, but not for long, because he slipped in a second finger.

Her response was feral. "Oh, yes," she growled. "Fuck me. Fuck me."

He wanted to scold her, to remind her he was not hers to command—but at the moment, he was. Seating three thick fingers inside, he tormented her swollen nub with his lips, worked her.

He hunted until he found the spot, the place deep inside where her nerves were raw and exposed and aching for his touch. He stroked her. Gouged at her. Besieged her.

All of a sudden, she stiffened. Every muscle clenched. Her walls seized around him in a mind-blowing vise. A hot rain, a wash of pleasure drizzled over his fingers.

He looked up. He had to see it—the expression on her face. It was sublime.

Ecstasy played over her features as he worked her with his fingers, stoking her orgasm, making her come again and again until she collapsed in a nerveless bundle in his arms.

Charlotte struggled to recover herself. She'd never come so hard.

In fact, calling those other things orgasms was almost a joke.

What Mark had done to her was unlike anything she'd ever known. And now he held her as her body quaked and quivered.

His arms were strong and warm. She felt the twitch of each muscle, the puff of each breath. The throb of his heart.

After a long while, he took her into his arms, carried her to the bedroom, and laid her on the bed. The pillows smelled of him. He left her side, giving her a moment to collect herself. He wasn't gone long. The bed dipped with his weight.

She opened her heavy lids and stared.

He smiled down at her, caressed her hair, her cheek. "Are you okay?"

"Yes." A laugh laced the word. She was more than okay. She was phenomenal.

"Are you ready to continue?" The surprise must have shown on her face, because he chuckled. "Oh, we're not done yet."

"We're not?"

"Hell, no." He held out something, a jumble of leather and soft chambray.

"What's this?"

"Restraints." He said it in a matter-of-fact tone that sent shivers slithering down her spine.

Lust reawakened, bubbled up.

"But only if you want to."

Did she? *Of course she did.* "Will you show me how to put them on?"

He did, slowly, cautiously, tracking her every reaction. "I'm going to tie you to the bed, Charlotte. And then I'm going to fuck you."

The thought should have horrified her, terrified her. It did not. She swallowed and met his warm brown gaze. "Okay."

Heat sizzled in his eyes. He yanked one of the leather cuffs tight, and after kissing the inside of her wrist, right on the fading scars of her recent ordeal, tightened the other. Then he hooked both restraints to the head of the bed. "Tug on them."

She did. They didn't budge.

"Still okay?"

She nodded.

He studied her for a moment, and then shifted. The muscles in his jaw clenched. Then, determinedly, he reached for the buttons of her blouse.

When the cool air hit her exposed nipples, she whimpered. But she remembered what he'd said. She kept her eyes on his face. And heavens, she loved looking at his face.

His head dipped. His warm, velvet mouth encased one nipple, then the other: lapping, licking, sucking. Delight assailed her with each minute caress. His palm drifted down her body, then back up under the hem of her dress. He found her core and stroked diligently. Before long she was writhing again. This time, with her hands bound, the feelings were even more intense. He could have his way with her—do anything—and she couldn't stop him. The knowledge liquefied her. Dampness seeped down her cleft.

When she was panting and writhing, he stood and ripped off his trousers. She gasped at the absolute beauty of his body. His briefs followed with no preamble.

Charlotte choked on her breath as his cock, hard and heavy, sprang free. He was thick, fat, and long, and she ached to feel him inside her. "Oh please," she whispered.

"Spread your legs." His voice was rough, like he was on the very edge of his control, like he was desperately reining himself in.

She let her thighs steal apart, revealing herself.

He raked his fingers through his thick hair and groaned. "Jesus, Charlotte. I've wanted this since the moment I saw you."

"I've wanted it too. Please. Fuck me, Mark."

* * *

Her words sent him over the edge, hurtling out of control. He yanked open the drawer of the bedside table, pulled out a condom, and slipped it on with trembling fingers. Then he knelt on the bed and levered over her. Without another word, he slipped inside.

She was tight. The sensation of his aching cock easing into her sopping cunt nearly unmanned him. She spread her legs further apart. He bit back a snarl of satisfaction as she tightened around him even more.

"Fuck me," she demanded.

And he lost his mind.

No longer able to take it slow, Mark pulled out and slammed back into Charlotte's warm and welcoming body. Shards of delight pierced his body as he thrust deep and deeper still.

Hard, hot, and fast, he fucked her, sluicing in and out at a dizzying pace. He couldn't get enough, didn't want it to ever end. She squeezed his length with each withdrawal, opened to him on every thrust. Her cries, her sharp gasps, her moans in his ear drove him on to darker insanity.

Too soon, he felt the pressure build. He closed his eyes, held his breath, and tried to force it back down, to hold it off.

But then she lifted her head and captured his lips. Nibbled on his tongue. Sucked it in. And the world exploded.

She came with him, clutching him, writhing beneath him and around him, taking him with her to ever more dizzying heights. Delirium cascaded in this soul as come jetted from him in a scalding rush.

It took a while for him to recover. He'd never known such absolute bliss.

And he knew why.

Because it was her.

Because it was Charlotte.

He released her at once, massaging and kissing her wrists. "So...is that something you might like to try again, some-time?"

She met his gaze with a serene smile. Her response delighted him.

"Oh yes, Sir. Yes."

HOOK ME UP

Adele Dubois

I'd give my right nut for a hot cup of coffee and breakfast," Knox Bennett said to his partner Frank Johnston as they unfastened their helmets and facemasks and loaded them into the truck. Their fire-retardant hoods came off next. "Then I want a shower and about ten hours' sleep." It would be an hour—at least—before he could take those small comforts.

Soot streaked his face, making him look like a blue-eyed raccoon, and stuck to his turnout coat, pants, and boots like paint splatter. Knox groaned as he climbed into the cab of Engine Number 6 on weary legs and started the engine. They'd pulled another all-nighter in a neighboring community where an arsonist had torched a second row of houses. It had taken ladders from four adjacent towns to put the fires out. "At least we have beds to go home to. It's a shame about all those families."

Frank buckled his seatbelt, riding shotgun. "When the FBI catches the bastard, I want to kick his ass before they haul him away." He emphasized his point with a terse nod of his dark head.

"Get in line." Knox turned right at the next intersection and headed south. Their station sat smack in the middle of apple-orchard country in southeastern Pennsylvania. The trees were just beginning to bud, and in another month apple blossoms would decorate every neighborhood in town. Just the sight of his home-town in the distance eased the tension in his neck and the kinks in his shoulders. Knox had never lived anywhere else and couldn't imagine ever wanting to leave Appleton. A wife, a few kids, and a promotion to captain would make life here just about perfect.

The flash of something out of sync with the earth-toned landscape slid past his peripheral vision, and he eased his foot off the accelerator by reflex. "Did you see that?" Knox checked his mirrors, tapped the brakes, and slowed.

"See what, bro?" Frank stretched to look outside his window.

"That slash of purple inside the old apple tree we passed back there. Like something was falling." Knox pulled over. "My gut tells me something isn't right."

"Turn around when I give the go." Frank hopped out of the truck and walked around to direct traffic.

Only two cars passed; the residential neighborhood was calm. Frank gave the all-clear and Knox reversed the fire truck with a three-point turn. The backup signals pierced the still morning air. Frank hopped on the rear and held the ladder as Knox moved forward.

Several houses down, Knox found what he was looking for—a tidy lawn with the oldest apple tree he'd ever seen growing from the center. A modest white house stood in its shade.

Knox got out of the truck and stood on the sidewalk, craning his neck to inspect the apple branches, while Frank came up behind him. Knox heard the sobs at the same time he spied the purple patch near the tree's highest limb.

Knox pointed. "There."

Adrenaline kicked in, erasing his earlier weariness. He ran to the truck to grab a hook and a coil of rope and bolted into the yard.

Lexi Wentworth sobbed and swore, scolding her kitten for getting them into this predicament. "Naughty Ginger for climbing up this tree," she said, trying again to right herself where she hung upside down.

She'd only cracked the front door open for a teensy second, to slip a birthday card for her mother into the mailbox, when Ginger had bolted through. Lexi had thought she could catch the tabby and bring her back inside without much fuss. How far could a kitten run up a tree?

Unfortunately, Lexi found the answer dressed in nothing but a hip-length, see-through purple nightie and matching thong above her bedroom slippers, which had since fallen off. Why she'd let her friend talk her into buying this getup, she'd never know. Becky said fantasy was good for the soul. Well, her soul was fine. Pretty much. Her sex life was the part that sucked.

Lexi's left leg had gotten stuck above the knee in forked twin limbs twisted with vines, and she'd toppled backward against the trunk. Bark dug into the small of her back and bare buttocks and dizziness swam as blood rushed to her head. Her nightgown hung upside down on her body, baring her breasts and abdomen to the birds and sky.

She tried to hoist herself up by pushing off two lower branches, but succeeded in merely arching her back. The lift offered muscle support and relief from the scratchy bark, but little else. She brushed the hem of her nightie from her face and tucked the garment under her chin. Her tabby mewled beside her, every hair on its slender body standing straight as a thistle.

"Poor kitty," she murmured. "You're more frightened than me."

To take pressure off her trapped leg and offer some leverage, Lexi reached for an overhead branch. She sighed as the maneuver reduced the pull to her knee. The reprieve was short-lived; the branch snapped off in her hand and sent her reeling back against the tree trunk. "Ow!"

The nightie slipped into a pool around her neck and chin, exposing her bare torso to the morning breezes. She might as well give up smoothing it over her breasts; it would only fall down again. Who the hell would see her, anyway?

The realization that no one might find her prickled her spine like a blast of cold needles. The half-acre lots in her neighborhood offered a great deal of privacy. Her nearest neighbors had already gone to work. Unless she started screaming at the top of her lungs, no one would know where to find her.

Terror struck and Lexi's tears welled. Her knee throbbed. Had she broken her leg? She counted off the weeks until the school year ended. If she had, she'd have to finish the marking period limping around her third grade classroom on crutches.

Assuming she got rescued. What if no one came?

She found her voice then and shouted for all she was worth. "Help! Somebody help me!" Perspiration dotted her temples as panic set in. "I need help!"

To her amazement, a husky, reassuring voice answered. "Try not to move. I'll be right up."

She must have grown delusional. The blood rushing from her feet to her brain had turned her mind to oatmeal. The most gorgeous man she'd ever laid eyes on moved into her line of sight and stood at the base of her apple tree. He had corn-colored hair and looked up at her with the eyes of an angel. The soot on his cheeks and chin couldn't camouflage the stunning face beneath.

A firefighter dressed in full regalia.

She watched, slack-jawed and filled with hope, as he pulled off his yellow-striped coat to reveal the dark T-shirt beneath. Even upside down she could see his trim waist and the way his tanned biceps flexed when he moved. She watched him pick tools off the ground—a circle of rope and a long-handled hook with an axe on the opposite side. In one smooth motion, he lifted the rope to his shoulder and clutched the hook as he began to climb.

That's when she remembered her naked breasts and the purple lace thong she barely wore.

Knox stared up at the woman caught in the apple tree in total disbelief. It wasn't just the jam she'd gotten herself into that surprised him, but the rescue fantasy she presented that pumped duel shots of liquid energy into his system. She was every fireman's wet dream. How was he supposed to remain professional and clearheaded while wearing a raging hard-on?

The higher he climbed, the more beautiful the woman became. Her skin looked smooth and soft to the touch. Long, honey-colored hair trailed beneath her like ripples in a pond. She stared at him over one shoulder with frightened but shining golden eyes. The look tore a hole through his gut.

He tried to be a gentleman and avert his eyes from her magnificent breasts and belly. Too late. He'd already noted every incredible curve and hollow, including the sexy gold ring at her navel. For the rest of his life he'd remember the way this extraordinary woman looked in this moment. Her image would be tattooed on his brain the way her rescue would become the firehouse tale that marked him as a man and defined his career.

None of that mattered now. All that counted was the help he could provide. His mind clicked through procedures until he processed the necessary steps to take her down safely. Since nothing in the manual covered this situation, he'd have to improvise. He hung the coil of rope on a stub and set the hook on a limb.

Knox noted no obvious serious injuries; the woman appeared calm, though he hadn't ruled out shock. "I've got you," he said. "Let me guide your hands to a supporting branch until I can get you down, okay?"

The woman blinked her understanding and offered a small nod. Her eyes shone with tears.

Knox held her wrists while she followed his lead.

As he maneuvered the woman's hands to a secure spot, something spit and hissed in his direction. Knox spotted a kitten and stifled a smile: no one from his firehouse had ever rescued a cat from a tree. "Let's get kitty safely out of the way so that I can focus on you."

"Her name's Ginger," the woman replied.

He reached for the frightened cat with one hand while he whispered words of encouragement.

The kitten mewed and licked his fingers after he scooped her up.

"Good girl."

Knox called down to his partner. "Frank! Take care of this cat, will you?" He leaned down and handed over the pet as Frank climbed up. Knox blocked the woman's nakedness from his partner's view as best he could. Her vulnerability stirred his protective instinct more than usual. "She could use a blanket when I bring her down." He asked for a couple of other things and turned back to the woman.

"Let's get that pressure off your leg." He drove the axe into the tree, then uncoiled the rope and looped it around a limb and the hook to create a makeshift pulley.

Knox climbed up to straddle a limb directly above the woman's trapped leg and tied the free end in a slipknot around his waist. Then he leaned down to cradle the woman in his arms.

The intimate contact of her warm, soft body against his forged a connection that struck his soul like a physical ache. Though he'd always been empathetic to fire victims, he rarely met the property owners whose flames he'd extinguished. This rescue became personal the moment the woman leaned into his shoulder.

He raised her into a sitting position. As he did, he lowered her nightgown over her breasts and belly to restore her privacy. The sheer fabric offered little of that, but she smiled at him in appreciation. The warm gold flecks in her eyes drew him in and he fought back an almost irresistible urge to kiss her. "I'm Knox. What's your name?"

"Alexis Wentworth. I'm called Lexi."

"Okay, Lexi. I'm going to slip the rope around us both and then hoist you up so that I can free your leg. Is that all right?"

Lexi nodded.

Knox continued to support her with one arm while he extended the loop around her torso with the other and pressed her tightly to his chest.

The moment her body touched his, the sweet scent of strawberries on freshly washed skin replaced the smell of smoke and soot that clung to him. Her soft breasts and the tips of her nipples caused his muscles to tense at the friction. He inhaled her fragrance—and then reprimanded himself to stay on task. Lexi might be beautiful and sexy as hell, but the job and her safety came first.

The piercing sound of Engine Number 6 backing into the front yard with Frank at the wheel came right on cue.

Knox spoke so that Lexi could hear. "On the count of three,

I'm going to pull you up." He studied her eyes for reassurance that she was ready. Satisfied, he began the count and heaved.

Their combined weight tested the hook's tensile strength until the pulley quivered. Knox tightened his hold and felt Lexi's heartbeat rise as the axe vibrated against the tree trunk.

He moved with more urgency then, throwing every ounce of his strength into the motion. Though his body ached from hours at the overnight crime scene and his muscles strained to the breaking point, Knox refused to falter.

When Lexi reached the fork that trapped her, Knox helped her hook her free leg over one limb. She sat upright and leaned a shoulder against the trunk while she held on, though her hampered knee made the pose awkward.

Knox pulled the axe free after adjusting his position and then retied their makeshift harness. "I'm going to have to chop it off. Do you mind?"

Lexi's eyes widened, and she shrieked for the first time since he'd climbed up to meet her. "You want to cut off my leg?" Her pallor turned white as paper.

Knox resisted a smirk. "No, the limb trapping your leg. It's got to go. Its twin will hold you. I'll work from the area above. You'll be fine."

She visibly relaxed, fear and trust mingling with relief in her expression. "Do I have to remind you to be careful with that thing?"

This time, he did smile. "I wouldn't think of damaging your leg." Her long, slender, magnificent leg. He wondered if she took ballet or yoga lessons. Suddenly those classes didn't seem so dumb.

Knox chopped the limb away a safe distance above her knee, cleared the vines, and tossed the debris to the ground. With care, he lifted her leg over the stump to free her.

She winced but didn't cry out during the extraction. Though her leg had bruised and become swollen, it didn't appear to be broken. He would take her to the hospital as a precaution.

The engine rumbled below them and the sounds of a hydraulic lift preceded the appearance of a white cherry picker.

Knox loosened their tether, stepped into the cab of the cherry picker, and as it lowered, lifted Lexi into his arms. She wrapped her hands around his neck and smiled up at him with admiration in her gorgeous golden eyes.

"Your chariot awaits, miss." The guys would call him a dick for the rest of his life if they knew he'd said that. Knox let the rope fall past his waist to the cab floor and kicked it away as they descended into the front yard. The way Lexi looked up at him made his words seem just right. Screw the guys and what they might think. He was the one holding the beautiful lady in his arms.

Knox grinned down at her. "I've always wanted to say that to a woman."

Three weeks later...

The captain stuck his head into the firehouse kitchen, where the crew had thrown an impromptu celebration for the arsonist's capture. "Bennett! Someone here to see you." His thick eyebrows rose and fell with the announcement, and a smirk lifted a corner of his mouth. The look gave tacit permission for everyone to check out Knox's visitor.

Chairs pushed back from the table and a handful of guys, including Frank, stood to watch from the doorway as Knox made his way into the main room.

Though he tried to control it, a spring lifted his step and hurried him forward when he spotted Lexi. She looked sexy as ever, in tight jeans and a pullover top that showed off her curves. He hadn't seen her since the day of her rescue, but had thought about her a million times.

He wanted to tell her she was the most beautiful woman he'd ever seen, and he wished he could have called her after taking her home from the emergency room that day. But the captain was the only person authorized to contact victims after the fact.

So instead of telling her how much he'd hoped she'd find him, and how happy he was to see her, he merely smiled and said "Hey."

The smile she returned eased any doubts that her feelings weren't reciprocal. She held out a large plate of cupcakes that he'd barely noticed. "I made these for you—to thank you, and the others, of course." She glanced over at the kitchen doorway where his buddies lingered, making no bones about staring. "I guess they heard about my purple nightie," she whispered.

"Not from me."

"Maybe these cupcakes will give us some privacy."

"Good thinking. Be right back." He delivered the baked goods amid wolf whistles and pats on the shoulder. "Eat, guys. Behave."

He led Lexi outside to a patch of lawn in the side yard where they could be alone. He stood close, noting that she didn't step back. "No crutches. I'm glad you're okay."

"I only needed them for a week because of the pulled muscles. I was lucky."

"Yeah. The captain gave me the update."

Her brow creased, and the sparkle in her eyes turned to accusation. "I thought I might hear from you directly. All the care you showed me at the hospital before you drove me home—I thought some of that might have been personal." The hitch in her voice offered the proof he needed that their connection hadn't been one-sided. The last thing the department needed was a...misunderstanding. He wrapped his hands around her waist and pulled her closer.

She stared up into his eyes while she eased against him.

"Regulations. Believe me, I wanted to show up at your door a thousand times." He ran his thumbs over the curves of her hips. "Since I couldn't, I did the next best thing."

"What was that?" Her stunning golden eyes narrowed with doubt.

"I asked the captain to mention how much I love cupcakes."

She draped her arms over his shoulders and leaned into the kiss he brought to her mouth. Her lips tasted supple and warm and sweet, better than any fantasy he'd imagined. He pictured her bare breasts with their mouthwatering nipples and the gold belly-button ring he wanted to poke with his tongue.

The next thing he knew, he'd pressed her back against the side of the firehouse and picked her up by the seat of her pants.

She wrapped her legs around his waist while he rubbed and squeezed her ass, remembering how perfect it had looked in a thong. His erection sought the sweet spot between her legs and pressed while she dug her fingers into his hair.

He kissed her until her pretty lips became flushed and swollen. Then, reluctantly, he put her down and took a step back before he broke every decency law in the book.

Knox brushed stray hairs off her forehead with his fingers. "I want to know all about you. Let's go out for dinner after my shift. Anyplace you want."

"I'd like that."

Her eyes sparkled when she looked at him this time and his spirit soared. He knew with absolute certainty that something good had started between them.

"Do you like to dance? We can do that, too. Tomorrow night

we'll go somewhere else. Bowling. The movies. I want to spend time with you. Often."

Exclusively. But he'd save that discussion for later.

Lexi ran her hands down the front of his tee shirt before letting him go. She looked up with a half-smile. "Let's do all those things. But Saturday night, we'll stay in. My house."

Lexi lit another candle and wondered what the hell had gotten into her. She'd invited Knox over for sex without hesitation. Deprivation *had* made her crazy.

Deep down, she knew that was a lie. She'd wanted him from the moment she saw him. When Knox initiated her rescue, she'd sensed his goodness. His *decency*. So few of the men she'd met lived up to that standard. Her intense sexual attraction merely accelerated the inevitable.

With Knox, she knew she was safe and free to let go. No other man had made her feel that way.

The doorbell rang. Lexi adjusted the bodice of her new white camisole and ran her fingers over the band of its matching thong. She smoothed her hair and took a last look around the living room. Candles on the coffee table issued a soft glow. Light snacks waited in the fridge. Background music played low.

Ready.

Knox grinned from his side of the threshold, taking in every inch of her like a long cool drink in hot sand.

She stared back at him, dressed in full uniform and holding a bottle of wine, and wondered if he was naked under his turnout pants and coat. Dear God, she hoped so.

"Someone call about a fire, Miss?"

She led him inside, set the wine on the coffee table, and kissed him, standing on tiptoes.

He kissed her back with passionate yet natural ease, as if they'd been together for months.

In one fluid motion he lifted her into his arms. "Bedroom?"

She pointed the way.

She'd lit candles there, too, so when he set her down on her queen-sized bed, their bodies shimmered with a lustrous glow. He stood over her at the edge of the mattress.

Lexi's heart pounded while she waited to see what he'd do next. She licked her lips in anticipation.

His nostrils flared at the sight of her tongue. He unclipped his helmet and laid it at the bottom of the quilt. Light flickered in his startling blue eyes, adding intensity to his already-handsome face.

She got up on her knees at the side of the bed and found the closures on his coat, starting at the bottom. *Pop.* The first one opened. She unhooked the next. Lexi stuck her hand inside the flap, hoping for skin instead of another layer of clothing.

Ahh. Her hand brushed the tight flesh of his stomach. His muscles contracted at her touch. *Pop.* Lexi opened another closure, then another, alternately running her hands over his bare chest and pinching his nipples while continuing her climb. When the coat hung open, she pushed it off his broad shoulders and watched as he eased it down and let it fall to the floor.

The sight of his naked torso looked better than she'd hoped. Knox had toned his body with obvious care, but without the excessive vanity she'd seen at the gym. A sprinkling of pale hair grew over his gorgeous pecs and taut stomach. Her gaze followed the darker line disappearing into his pants. Her fingers itched to discover what waited inside.

Before she could unhook his turnouts, he lifted her to her feet on the bed and pressed his face to the swell of her breasts. He

kissed the skin above her camisole with a heady mix of rever-
ence and lust. In an instant, he pulled the fabric over her head
and tossed it away.

He ravished her then; that was the only way to explain what
happened next. Lexi gave herself over to Knox without hesitation as he explored every inch of her body with fingers and
tongue, bringing her to the brink and back a dozen times over.
His sole attention to her pleasure proved once again how selfless
he could be.

Lexi could be generous, too. She pulled at the waistband of
his pants. "I want to see you."

Her lover stripped naked then, letting the coarse fabric of his
turnouts run over his hips and down his long, sturdy legs.

Lexi sucked in an appreciative breath at the sight of his ready
cock. "Nice." Not too big or too small, just the right size to bring
her bliss. She stroked his length and licked his shaft, tasting the
silken texture of his skin and inhaling his unique scent. She
brought her lips over the crown and pulled him into her mouth
until he rested a hand against her jaw in gentle warning and
pulled back with a hiss between his teeth. He moved to the bed
and rolled down the quilt.

Lexi scooted onto the bottom sheet and watched while Knox
tucked his helmet beneath the outer layers of covers to create
a mound near the edge of the mattress. He inclined his head.
"That's for you."

He guided her onto her back, horizontally across the bed,
with her hips lifted high on his padded helmet.

She spread her legs and watched him savor the sight of her
damp, open pussy.

"You're so beautiful," he whispered.

Knox knelt between her legs and ran his fingers over her
tender folds, exposing her fully erect clit. His thumb circled and

pressed the delicate bud, taking her closer to orgasm with each revolution.

When he pressed his mouth to her center and slid his tongue inside her, Lexi cried out. She plunged her hands into his hair while he licked and sucked her clitoris until she begged him to take her over the edge.

The crackle of paper followed her plea as Knox rolled on a condom.

Lexi dug her heels into the bed and angled her hips in anticipation.

Knox thrust into her, pulled, and thrust again deeply, holding her by the waist as they moved in syncopated time.

How could she have known they'd fit perfectly, as if they belonged together? His cock slid over just the right places, and she climaxed while she writhed with her release.

Knox fucked her harder and faster while she came, and cried out soon after. When his muscles relaxed, he kissed her belly and licked the gold loop at her navel. His tongue dragged over her solar plexus until he reached her breasts and nipples. Finally, his lips met hers for a tender kiss.

Ginger hopped up on the bed while they lay in the afterglow, wrapped in each other's arms.

Knox reached out to pet the kitten. "I have you to thank for this, little puss. Get used to me hanging around." He kissed Lexi and stroked her skin.

She marveled at how lucky she'd been to get stuck in her apple tree. As Knox moved to make love to her again, Lexi nibbled his earlobe and murmured, "You made clever use of your helmet. Next time you come over, let's see what you can do with your coil of rope."

Knox laughed. "Anything for you, gorgeous."

BIG TRUCKS

Lynn Townsend

The tones went off at the bottom of the tenth.

"Goddamn it!" Steve Tillery jumped to his feet, throwing his Cardinals cap to the ground in disgust.

Amy Whitaker, Engine 31's driver, unfolded from the battered, stained sofa.

Steve was acutely aware of the brief contact between their shoulders as she brushed past him. He paused, mid-alarm and mid-frustration over missing the game, to watch the curve of her ass and the smooth shift of thigh as she was out the door toward the stable.

"There's no good time for a fire, Steve-o!" Chris Neily responded. "The Rangers won't whip your boys' asses any worse if you're not watching."

"If someone's burned the freaking popcorn, I swear, I'm—"

"Can the chatter, boys," the captain called out. "I'm seeing too many lips flapping and not enough asses and elbows!"

"Yes, Captain," Steve and Chris responded, in stereo.

Then it was nothing but boots and gear and getting on the steed. Banter came in short, limited doses, at least until the trucks were rolling, sirens screaming as the dispatcher gave more details: structure fire, eight homes in the one building, with two similar-sized buildings in danger of going up.

"Step on it, Whitaker!" Voices crackled and popped in Steve's earbud as the chatter grew more animated.

Amy acknowledged with a brief "Gotcha," before she slammed the pedals of Engine 31 down, her strong, confident hands on the wheel. She drove like a racer, smooth and unhesitating, jamming thirty thousand pounds of truck, water and equipment onto the streets with confidence.

Chris rocked out of his seat briefly—of course he hadn't buckled in. "Damn woman drivers," he joked, straightening his gear.

"You can always get out an' walk, Neily," Amy snapped, squeezing between an SUV loaded with half the local soccer team and one of those little electric commuter cars.

Steve winced, but Amy was—smart-assed remarks aside—a remarkable jockey.

"One of these days," she muttered, flaring the horns at some ass on the phone, "I'mma talk Chief Bradbury into escorting us to a fire. Let the boys in blue hand out tickets to all the Kmart shoppers."

"Yeah, let me know how that works out for ya," Steve muttered.

Smoke and the angry orange reflections of fire stabbed up accusingly at the starry sky, outlining the silhouettes of trees and buildings.

"Four minutes twenty," the captain barked out as 31 pulled up to the emergency. "Nice work."

The crew scrambled out of the truck, Hinkley on the deck

gun. Steve grabbed an IFEX handheld from the rack, buckling
his helmet one-handed.

"Cops are already on-scene," Amy reported. "Pushing the
crowd back. Possible rescues on the second floor." Amy always
called them rescues, always treated any trapped victims as if
they were already safe and just didn't know it yet.

"Goin' in," Steve said. "Someone find a resident, get me a
head count."

Steve was through the door and into the staircase before
word trickled in: three kids left behind by the babysitter and the
babysitter's boyfriend.

"Boyfriend dragged her out," Amy said. "She's hysterical,
but he was smart. Ain't no place in a fire for a teenage girl."

"Amen to that." He'd seen it too many times. In a panic,
mother leaves the house, then goes back in. Rescue gets the
kids, but the mom's gone. Golden rule of fire: once you get out,
stay out.

Steve led the charge into the burning apartment, kicked the
door down, and sensed more, then heard Chris at his back.
Uncle Buck Cartwright and his nephew, Kyle, brought up the
rear, humping the hose with them.

Steve damn near tripped over the first kid, a girl in a filthy,
torn T-shirt and diaper, curled up near the door. "Kyle!" He
scooped the baby up and handed her over. Only Kyle's third live
fire, and Cartwright's sister Angela had already chewed their
asses once for letting the boy take risks. "Get her out, I'll check
the bedrooms!"

Kyle was going to have to grow up sometime. The Cart-
wrights had been founding members of the station, back in
1902, but no one could tell Angela that. She'd married into the
family. Fuck it. There'd probably be a picture-snapper out there
with the looky-loos to get the boy on the front page, carrying

the baby out the door. Maybe that would get Angie on the truck with everyone else.

"Roof's ablaze," Hinkley said. "14 and 9 are on scene soaking down the neighbors."

"Someone's insurance is gonna scream blue murder," Chris said.

"Lives first, paperwork later," Steve chanted. "Get me some water in here!" He pushed into the living area. The television was the only recognizable thing left, and it was pouring white smoke; the sofa and chairs were lumps of misshapen ash and smolder. Chris flipped the chairs and shoved the burning sofa away from the wall; kids did the damnedest things in a fire. Hid under tables, in closets, behind dressers.

Chris peeled off, kicking in the toasted door to the bathroom with one booted foot. "Got one here," he reported.

That kid was sopping wet, the water steaming off his skin as Chris wrapped him in a towel. He must have filled the tub. "Chessie! Chessie!" The boy screamed, pointing back toward the deepest part of the apartment, where the fire was worst.

"Go, go!" Steve yelled. "I'm on the third." He hoped. "We'll get Chessie out."

The bedroom was hell in a kettle. Flames wreathed the walls. Smoke was dense and black, obscuring his vision. Any kid in here...

Steve shook his head. He stopped in the door, careful. The floor seemed solid enough. He glanced around, letting his eyes rest on each area of the room for a few seconds. Bed was so much char. Bookshelves, the twisted remains of a space heater. One for the fire marshal to prod at, he expected. Closet door was open, there was nothing in there but flaming clothes and toys... toys... He shifted his gaze. The toy box—solid wood with cracking, faded paint—huddled just below the window. He strode across the room, lifted the lid.

Chessie was in there, blanket over her head, pink My Little Pony footie pajamas on. She didn't move when he lifted her, and in the strange darkness of the fire-bright room, shadows throwing crazed sparks into the air, he couldn't tell if she was breathing. Behind him the doorframe collapsed, along with a fair amount of ceiling and roofing tile.

"Amy!" Steve bellowed into his helmet mike. "Need you, babe. Get me a ladder up here, second floor!"

"On it!"

Her voice was music in his ears. Keeping the girl tight to his chest, he cracked the window. Tricky bit of work, with windows. If you opened them, you could get out, but there was also the risk of fanning the flames. Here, he didn't think there was much choice. "Got a fuckin' traffic cone in my way. Goddamn cops." Steve peered out the window to watch the cop scramble back out of the patrol car to move it away.

"I got the kid here," Steve said, "which is making suppression all kinds of unreasonably difficult."

"Get your panties out of your ass," Amy said. "I'm coming."

The tower came up, Hinkley already climbing up like a pirate's monkey. "I got the kid, you get your ass down here," he said, holding one arm out for Steve's bundle. "If we're lucky on this one, we can save the basement."

Just before he threw his legs over the windowsill, Steve heard Amy snort into her headset. "Yeah, save the basement for a swimming pool."

"How ya doing, hero?" Amy threw a towel at Steve as he crossed out of the locker room, hair dripping down his T-shirt, feet bare.

"Whose Kool-Aid you been drinking? Thought that reporter was going to cream her jeans for the interview with Kyle."

"Yeah, yeah, brush it off."

"I don't do the job to get medals pinned on my chest," Steve said. "It's not about that. It was never about that." Steve toweled his hair vigorously, suppressing the smile that teased at his mouth as Amy danced back out of the way of flung water droplets.

Amy perched on one of the stools near the coffee maker. She poured and handed him a mug.

Black, viscous crap. Ah, the glamorous life of a hero. He drank it anyway. Another hour on shift, and then he still had to drive home. But the four days off would be sweet even if they weren't over a weekend.

"So what is it about? For you?"

"Someone's gotta do it," Steve said. "And since I can... What about you? What are you here for?"

Amy ignored the question. "Is it worth it? Everyone says that's why Lindsey left you. The job. You even get to see your kid this weekend? Play a little catch?"

"More like hack up zombies," Steve said. "Kids don't want to play ball anymore. They wave controllers at the TV."

"Get off my lawn, old man," Amy smirked.

"It's hard for some people," Steve said. He wasn't angry with Lindsey. Not really. Although he could have done without paying huge legal fees to defend his right to see Cody more than twice a year. "Having someone you care about risking his life all the time."

"There are better ways to cope," Amy said. She hooked her feet around the legs of her barstool, cuddling her coffee mug without actually tasting it. She grimaced and stretched her fingers.

"Still gripping the wheel too hard?" Steve plucked one slender, calloused hand from around the warm ceramic and pressed his thumbs to the sore spot in the center of her palm.

She groaned and put the cup down, contents still unsampled. Smart woman.

"That feels heavenly," she said. She shook her head back, the weight of her gold-blond hair seeming too heavy for her slender throat. Amy stayed that way, hair swinging loose over her back, eyes closed. She licked her lips in appreciation, a few low groans passing between her lips as he massaged first one hand, then the other.

He moved closer, holding her arm to his chest as he worked his thumbs into sore muscles.

"You slipped up today."

"Hmmm?" He wasn't exactly listening, too busy watching the play of sensual responses on her face, his body heating from her nearness.

"How about we not play this game anymore?" Amy opened her eyes, a rich, creamy smile painting her mouth as she took note of how close he was, their faces separated by nothing more than the merest whisper. "Let's just admit we like each other and see what happens."

"Amy..." Steve tried to take a step back and suddenly her hand tightened on his. He could have broken her grasp, but freeing himself from her gaze was impossible. "We work together."

"You want me to quit my job before you'll admit you want me?"

"Hell no," Steve said. "We need you here."

"And you? What do you need?" She leaned closer still, until the heat of her breath was enough to drive him mad.

"This is a mistake," he said, stepping into the cradle of her thighs.

"Only if you actually get around to making it," she said, her voice breaking with a sound: half sob, half laughter.

He kissed her. The world could have burned, but for that moment, there was nothing else beyond her kiss. The silken taste of her mouth, the faint remnants of the fire-smell in her hair, her warm hands against his chest, the pressure of her thighs against his hips.

"Come on, hero," Amy whispered against his hair, "we probably shouldn't wait 'round here 'til next shift. The boys will want their engine degreaser."

Engine 31 was hosed down, fresh and clean already from the afternoon's adventure.

Amy spread her coat along the step-up into the cab. "If there's another fire..." she started, biting at her lip, suddenly uncertain.

"We'll be right here. Can't get much faster than that," Steve said, catching her mouth in another kiss and swallowing the rest of her words. He tugged her T-shirt up, hands on the sleek flesh of her back.

She arched as his fingers traced the path of her spine, tickling and caressing the small of her back. She was braless beneath and he couldn't resist the siren call of her breasts, licking a trail of fire over her stomach until his mouth closed over her stiffening nipple.

Amy's quick, clever fingers were on his belt, loosening the buckle and then popping open the buttons on his fly.

"Hey, slow down," Steve said, pulling her hand up to his mouth and nipping the tips of her fingers. "Where's the fire?"

Amy snorted, a singularly unfeminine noise. "Is it mandatory," she asked, "for every firefighter in the world to make that joke?"

Steve considered it, licking down her index finger and planting a kiss in the palm of her hand.

She shivered under his ministrations.

"Yeah, probably."

"Jerk."

"And yet you want me anyway."

"I always did have bad taste." Amy shrugged. She tugged off her T-shirt, dropping it to the floor.

"I don't know about that," Steve joked. He traced a line of kisses down her throat, along her collarbone, then returned to her nipple, teasing it erect with his tongue. "I think you taste pretty good." He nuzzled at the warm flesh under her breast, nibbled down her ribs, and tongued the ticklish spot over her hip until she was breathless and twisting in his arms.

This time, when she reached for his jeans, he let her, aching for her touch.

Her hand was quick, warm, the skin soft as she brushed against the flesh of his lower stomach. Muscles jumped and twitched along his belly and thighs, his cock hard inside suddenly-too-tight denim. She undid his buttons far too slowly, and he groaned aloud when she finally took him in hand.

She pushed his jeans down around his ankles and nudged him backward until he sat on her coat, feeling the muted prickle of boot-grip steel under the rugged canvas.

With a lithe elegance that heated his blood to boiling, Amy stepped out of her own jeans, revealing long, shapely legs and a pair of white granny panties the likes of which could tent half the station.

"Oh, very sexy," he growled, low in his throat, and pulled her to him for a fierce kiss, tasting her tongue, devouring her mouth.

Amy's fingers came up to cup the base of his skull and rasped against his brutally short hair. "You want sexy underwear, you have to take me out. You want a quickie against the steed, you settle for what don't ride up my ass while I'm working."

Steve grinned against her mouth, then nipped her chin lightly. "I'm not complaining. They look—you look—amazing."

Amy climbed onto the stairwell with him, knees wide, bracketing his thighs. She gripped the rails and raised her hips.

Steve curled an arm around her back to support her, his other hand wandering down the flat plane of her belly and down, fingers teasing around the pale triangle of hair.

She squirmed, twisting against him, her thighs rubbing against the length of his cock.

He swallowed hard, forced himself to go slow. His cock had other opinions about that and let him know with a twist of almost-pain along his stomach.

"There, there," Amy whispered, shifting her hips again, directing his roaming fingers. She adjusted her grip on the rail, thrusting her breasts forward.

He took one offered nipple, biting gently and licking at the very tip. The folds of her labia were swollen and he teased the plump skin there, running the nail of his thumb lightly along the split as she wriggled against his fingers.

Eyes closed, she leaned back hard against his arm, nearly bowed backward, her blond hair tickling against his knees and calves.

He dropped a hot, wet kiss along her belly, then spread her folds, finding the tiny bud of sensation within, flicking it neatly with his fingertips.

She spasmed against him almost immediately, the damp skin growing hotter, wetter. Her female scent, rich and pungent, teased his nostrils.

Steve rubbed his thumb along her clitoris, pressing up and around, circling and brushing against the tender skin, quick then slow as her breath raced in and out of her lungs. He watched her face, his own wanting barely contained as he teased, bringing her closer and closer, then backing off, almost grinning at her soft mewls of frustration.

She raised up, pulling herself closer to him, trapping his hand between their bodies. "Now, damn it," she ordered, biting the shell of his ear.

Her entrance was hot, soaking wet, over him. He curled his hand under her hip, lifted her ass. His cock pressed, eager and with a mind of its own, against her vestibule. He flicked his thumb again, awkward but effective, against her clitoris, rotating his hips slowly, rubbing the head of his cock against her flesh, just the head, just a tease, a taste, the faintest brush.

She convulsed against him. Her teeth shaped a fiery circle against his shoulder, biting down, stifling her scream against his skin, and at that moment he thrust into her, the paroxysms of her internal muscles tight and feverish over his aching shaft.

Amy twisted her hips, grinding down on him, bracing herself against the rails. The slide of flesh against flesh, not just up-and-down thrusting like he was accustomed to but a sliding, gliding spiral, her soaked, soft depths against his hard length, a molten dance of skin against skin.

"That's good," he said, gasping the words against her throat, beaded with sweat. He wrapped his arms around her, fingers biting into the small of her back, pulling her closer, closer. He wanted his whole self inside her, every fiber of his being. She was sweet, so sweet, and she shivered against him, mouth hot and wet against his shoulder, her gasps and moans music to his ear.

"I...yes, now...yes. More." She arched back, releasing the rails, trusting in his strength, her whole body going stiff and rigid against his, breasts thrust up, glistening with her sweat, hands fisted against her thighs as she trembled.

Her internal muscles gripped him tight as he thrust against

the wicked softness, once, twice, again, and she shuddered as he emptied himself into her. The sensation of heat and release, a tiny bundle of nerves at the base of his cock, expanded, a spark, an ember, and it rushed over him, body ablaze with that single sensation. It couldn't last more than an instant, and yet it did—forever in a perfect moment.

"Oh my," he said.

"Oh my, indeed."

They rested, a tangle of weary, sweaty limbs.

Her hair was a damp and stringy mess across her face and back.

He tasted the salt of her skin, kissing her throat and ear. "That was wonderful."

"I thought so," she responded.

"You never did tell me," he said.

"What?"

"Why you do it...why you're a firefighter."

"Oh, that's easy." Amy smirked. "I like big trucks, and I cannot lie."

LOST AND
FOUND

Nanette Guadiano

In every woman's life there comes a time when she has to
make the decision to truly live or merely exist. That time, for
me, came five months ago, with the passing of my thirty-sixth
birthday. It was like a switch had been flipped inside me.

Suddenly, my daily routines, my career, my friends, and my
lover weren't enough. The dreams of my youth (having someone
I couldn't live without, making babies, writing my novel, and,
fingers crossed, actually getting it published) were alive again
like a fire in my gut: a living, breathing entity, swallowing all
the oxygen around me, burning me. I told myself I didn't really
have a choice, but that wasn't entirely true. I could have given up
and accepted defeat; I could have chosen a life of mundanity, but
the hamster-in-a-wheel gig was killing me. I'd been a walking
corpse for far too long. So I made the decision to change things.

I broke up with Alejandro, my boyfriend of five years;
packed up my classroom for the last time at the end of May
without signing my contract for the next school year; sold my

little house for a small profit; donated everything I didn't need
or want to charities; and booked a one-way flight to Italy with
the plan of maybe never coming home.

Now here I am, in a tiny town called Forete, just minutes
from Verona. I've just arrived in a seventeenth-century Italian
villa that I've rented for the next three months. Long enough
to forget my past, long enough to dream of a future, and—I
hope—long enough to finish the novel I started ten years ago.
So why am I so afraid?

I open the windows, fresh air disturbing long-dormant dust
motes into frenetic swirls in clumps so large they could pass for
snowflakes. Birds chirp. Children play outside on bikes, their
Italian words like tinkling Baroque music on a harpsichord. I
take a deep breath and sigh. My armpits are wet; I'm exhausted,
jet-lagged, and afraid. What have I done?

On the corner is a small grocery store. My head throbs, but
there is no aspirin to be found. Grocery stores here sell only
groceries. If I want aspirin or tampons, I am told I have to find
a *farmacia*, a pharmacy. Life is slower here than back home,
where superstores have taken over, selling everything from
aspirin to tractors. Here, it's different. I am both annoyed and
comforted by this. I don't have a car and the hour is too late to
walk to the *farmacia*, which is three miles down the road, so
I choose a bottle of red wine in place of aspirin. Maybe it will
relax me enough to melt my headache. I grab some prosciutto,
grapes, and cheese for dinner and I'm off, back to the *aparta-
mento*, feeling more than just a little homesick.

Maybe dumping Alejandro was a bad idea. He had seemed
genuinely heartbroken when I ended it, said he couldn't understand why I was leaving him, why I was leaving it all. Didn't I
know he loved me? Really? If he loved me so much, he would
want the same things I wanted: marriage and children. But

Alejandro was content with the status quo, and I was tired of pretending that this life was enough.

I wanted things. What was so wrong with that? He had called me selfish. Ironic, considering our lovemaking had become as stale as day-old microwave popcorn. We had become a couple whose idea of kinky was me on top. And oral sex? Forget about it. Getting him to do it was like pulling teeth, and when he did I never came. I wanted passion—crazy, sexy sex. I wanted hair-pulling, mind-blowing, all-out fuck-fests. I would never have that with Alejandro. As if to clear my mental slate, I shake my head. I have to live in the moment. I'm in Italy, for god's sake.

I step off the sidewalk and begin to cross the street toward my rental. Out of the corner of my eye, I see a little boy kicking a ball. It bounces into the street and he darts out. My heart freezes in my chest. His mama shouts for him to stop, but he is quick, a little whirlwind of energy, a dizzying mass of light and curls. I turn to reach for him, dropping my bag of wine and olive oil. That's when I see the car speeding down the narrow street, going far too fast to stop in time. I don't even have time to scream, let alone go after him. His mama wails to Jesus. A screeching of brakes sounds, and I brace myself for the sound of death, but it does not come.

Slowly, I open my eyes. A flurry of excitement bubbles all around me. The driver of the Maserati is out of his car, screaming in Italian, motioning with his hands like a ridiculous parody of Woody Allen. The mother runs to her child, who is in the arms of a very tall, very blond, very muscular man in running clothes. The man's eyes meet mine. They are blue, the color of the Italian sky, *il cielo azurro*: blue heaven. I look down at my feet, oil and wine pooling like blood around my shoes, like petulant children refusing to play together.

It's hard to settle down after the incident with the little boy. I have eaten too much cheese, and I wish more than anything I hadn't dropped that bottle of wine. The air is hot, but habits are hard to break, and I will not sleep with the windows open on a ground floor. I'm from the city and filled with American fears.

I spend a good couple of hours trying to write, but I am far too jetlagged, far too restless to sit still long enough to listen to the muses. I try sleeping, but I'm so damn hot, my sweaty T-shirt clings to my breasts. My mind drifts back to the hand-some stranger. He was clearly not Italian. His features were almost Nordic: high cheek bones, suntanned skin, light lashes, blond hair, and the sexiest dimple on his chin. The way he held that little boy, such protection, such expertise…and he'd been so fast, like rescuing people was second nature.

I feel a tug in my womb, a longing I haven't felt in ages. My fingers drift down to my underwear. Picturing his eyes on mine, his intense and piercing gaze, my fingers explore my cunt for the first time in a long while, slowly at first. I tease my opening with a forefinger. I'm so wet; my pulse pounds against my chest. So much desire; I had forgotten what it felt like for my body to long for completion. My fingers work quickly now, alternating between tiny frenetic movements against my clit to long strokes inside of my warmth. In and out, up and down, side to side; thinking of blue, blue eyes, I begin to forget the heat.

La Dolce Vita Trattoria, the sign says. Today, I am less jetlagged and in a much better mood, thanks to a good night's sleep and a little self-love. Maybe I will find an Italian lover while I'm here. I will have my cappuccino and then take a bus to Verona, do a little shopping, some people-watching. The lady at the counter does not speak English, so I reach into my college past as though for spare change and pull out what little Italian I remember. Together, we manage to successfully get me some pizza and a cappuccino.

Sitting by the window, I try to ignore the screeching of a Roman pop star singing "My Sharona" in Italian on the flat-screen television mounted to a wall. I sink my teeth into the pizza and close my eyes. The sensation is almost sexual, the cheese is so good melting in my mouth: warm, gooey. I don't know what's wrong with me. Everything is turning me on. My clit jumps at the memory of the night before. The bell over the door chimes, signaling another customer. I look up, cheese dripping out of my mouth, and I almost choke when I see my handsome stranger. He grins at my messy face, and I feel crimson flood my cheeks. I grab a napkin and wipe my mouth.

The woman at the counter knows him. Her face lights up and her tongue rattles off in Italian too fast for me to interpret. He returns the banter in her language, but I detect a familiar lilt...British, perhaps?

"You are new here, am I right?" He stands next to my table, a bottle of water in one hand and a delicious-looking pastry in his other.

I can't help but notice how masculine his hands are, fingers thick and calloused. Definitely British. He is dressed for a run. "I just got here yesterday," I say.

"May I?" He gestures to the seat in front of me.

I nod, my gaze drifting back to the woman with the punk hair and whiny voice.

"American?"

"Is it that obvious?" I say, turning to him.

He laughs. "Sorry, but this is Forete. Not many tourists here, usually the same old crowd. Locals. You get your tourists in Verona, of course, but this is a small little village. Not much to see here. So, yes, it's obvious." He says something to the woman behind the counter and she smiles her lovely Italian

smile. I understand the words *"bella," "donna," "Americana."*
But that's about all.

She brings over a bottle of red wine and two glasses.

"For yesterday." He smiles. "I couldn't help noticing you lost
yours."

"My wine. Yes. I thought that little boy…" I don't finish
the sentence but I see the gravity in his eyes. He thought so,
too. "You were so quick. I feel awful. I just closed my eyes and
braced myself."

"Yes, well. It was lucky, I suppose. The situation could have
ended quite badly."

I love his accent. I want to place my fingers over his lips as
he talks, trace his words with my fingers. His eyes darken as
though he's read my thoughts. I look away. "It was more than
luck. Are you a police officer?"

An edginess appears around his eyes—the eyes of a man who
has seen disaster and has known tragedy.

"No. I'm a fireman."

"Ah. I knew you had to be in the rescue business." I smile.
No mistaking the hardness around his eyes now. I have touched
a nerve. "Where do you work?"

"London. I'm on holiday."

"How long have you been here?"

"Four months."

"That's a long holiday."

"I suppose it is."

"I'm Anna."

"William. So, Anna, what are you doing here in Forete? Why
not Rome or Tuscany? That seems to be where Americans like
to vacation."

"I'm a writer. I wanted to immerse myself in Italian culture,
so I picked a place far enough away from the city but close

enough for comfort. For obvious reasons, I love Verona."

"A writer. What do you write?"

Now I am on edge. What do I tell him? *Nothing, of late?* "I'm working on a novel." Typical response for a victim of writer's block.

"You here with family?" he asks, a little too loosely.

He's fishing, and I want to bite. "I'm alone," I whisper.

"Oh," he says. He pours wine into our glasses, hands me one and holds his up for a toast. "To holidays." He smiles.

"Cheers," I say.

We finish the bottle and order another. Time passes quickly and before long, it's siesta—closing time.

The lady shoos us away politely.

"Where are you off to, lovely Anna?" he asks as we step outside.

"Back to the drawing board, I suppose," I say, and I actually mean it. Today I think I could write. I would start by describing the way the muscles in William's jaw move when he isn't talking, as though he's holding back the most important part of himself—the roughness around his edges. Next to describe the way his biker shorts hug the sinew and veins of his thighs, the way his hair curls at the ends, like a child's or an Italian cherub's. I could write about how I long to have him come inside of me, fill me with his elixir, and about the possibility of a future. I could write a lot of things.

"Could I walk you home?" he asks.

"Of course," I answer. I do not want this day to end.

We get to my front steps and I pause a moment to fumble for my key. Suddenly, I'm filled with the most overwhelming sense of despair. I don't want to write about the experience. I want to live it. "I don't suppose you'd want to come in for a bit," I hear myself say.

"I'd love to."

Once inside, I open the windows to let in fresh air. My hands shake with nervousness. What do I know about this stranger anyway? He could be a serial killer, a rapist. He could be married. I doubt the wisdom of my decision. He senses the change in me, stays where he is, leans against the wall, and sighs deeply.

"Maybe this is a bad idea," I say.

His eyes cloud over, hooded with desire. He moves forward, and suddenly I am afraid. I don't know him. Fantasy aside, this is dangerous. I feel my clit jump. I can't believe I'm turned on, my juices dripping like a percolator. What is wrong with me?

"Beautiful Anna," he whispers, voice husky with desire. "Aren't you tired of playing things so safely? I know I am. I saw it in your eyes yesterday. You're like me—tired of being afraid." The outline of his impressive erection presses against his biker shorts.

My legs tremble now. I want his cock inside of me. I want to squeeze my pussy muscles around it and feel him piercing me.

He reads my need, senses in me a kindred spirit. I am no longer afraid. He touches my face, tracing his finger along the muscle in my jaw, feeling it relax beneath his fingers. I don't know what tragedy he saw, what victim he didn't save, but it's there—the facts are all there in his body language like pictures next to entries in an encyclopedia.

I move my hand down his chest, feel his pectorals flex beneath my touch. He breathes heavily now, and I shake with delicious anticipation. My nipples strain against my bra, begging to be sucked. My hands move down to the elastic of his shorts; his erection jumps into my hand like an eel—throbbing and huge. I cannot wait any longer. I pull down his shorts and kneel in front of him like a worshipper, licking his shaft like an ice-cream cone. It is beautiful, thick, and veiny. He groans with desire as I take him in my mouth. I could come right now, the sensation feels so good. I move my head against him as though I'm bobbing for apples.

His hands are in my hair, and then he's pulling me up. Alejandro always made me finish. But William, apparently, likes to be teased. Swiftly, so swiftly I wonder if it's actually happening, he lifts me up, spins us both around, and falls into a chair so that I'm straddling his lap. A fireman's move, and I don't know if he does it with all the ladies, but damn if it isn't sexy.

He kisses me now, probing my mouth with his expert tongue. I grind against his erection frantically, feeling my desire rising. I am close to coming, but he is not about to let me. As he stands, he lifts me up, flips me over his shoulder like a ragdoll, and walks me to the bedroom. He throws me on the bed, pulls down my panties, gives me a good long stare, and then buries his face in my cunt. He licks me, flicking my clit from side to side expertly as he fingers me with two of those masculine fingers I had been coveting only moments before in the *trattoria*.

I'm almost there. I'm so wet, it's unreal. He begins to drink me, to suck my juices like he's eating a peach. The sound of his slurping takes me over the edge. I cry out as three of his fingers enter me, darts of fire exploding in my belly; for a moment, I leave my body. He lifts my blouse over my head, and I am amazed at how quickly I'm aroused again at the sight of his erection. I want to feel him, skin on skin. I reach out to pull up his shirt and he flinches and moves away.

"What's wrong?" I ask.

"Nothing," he whispers, shaking his head, unsure.

I see the burns from his belly button all the way up one side of his torso, like dark pink stucco on a white wall. Vulnerability is there in his face, and I wonder now what tragedy sent him to Italy on a four-month "holiday." He is beautiful, his burns a testament to his character and dedication to his profession. I reach out to touch him. I feel his intake of breath. My fingers move over his scars like they're reading Braille. I want this man more than I've ever wanted anyone. I lean over and kiss him there, trace his map of skin with my mouth. The healing wound is smoother than I expected.

He groans and pulls me up, turns me over, and slaps me on the ass.

My cunt is begging to be filled. "Please," I whisper, on the verge of tears.

"Please what? What is it you want me to give you, beautiful Anna?"

"You know," I say.

"I only know what you tell me," he says gruffly, delivering a series of spankings so hard and fast I'm embarrassed.

Alejandro and I never talked dirty. Whenever I tried, he shot me down as though I was some sort of degenerate. "I want it," I whisper.

"You want what?" He teases, sliding a finger inside of me.

A whimper escapes my mouth.

"Tell me, Anna. You can trust me. What is it you want? I'll give you whatever you want."

"I want your cock."

He breathes heavily now. He grabs my ass cheeks and squeezes them together.

My wetness runs down my inner thighs.

"Where do you want it?"

I feel his tongue inside my hole. He's fucking me with his tongue, squeezing my ass cheeks together. I grind against his mouth. "Inside of me. Please. I want your cock inside of me."

I feel him position himself behind me. He thrusts deep in

me and I cry out; one thrust and I am coming and coming and coming. He bucks against me, forcing me to ride out my orgasm; the movement fuels his desire. As soon as one wave subsides, another comes. He is magnificent. He slides a finger inside my asshole, and I am almost there again. Reaching beneath me, he fingers my clit.

The touch is too much; tears well in my eyes.

He flips me over, buries his face in my neck as he pounds me, unmercifully, his dick so hard I know he's about to come. He lifts his face to mine, and with two deep thrusts and an inhuman growl, he comes, his gaze never leaving mine.

For several moments, we lay there breathing heavily. Aftershocks tremble through my body. He reaches over, places a large hand over my left breast, and pulls me against his body.

My eyes close and I inhale his musk and maleness, surprised at my body's response to this stranger. I wonder why I ever felt afraid. I don't know him; still, I feel safe. I want to tell him everything about me, and want to know everything about him. But there is no hurry. I listen to the sounds of our breathing, of the birds outside my window and the children playing in the street. I feel my eyes grow heavy as sleep covers me like a blanket. I relax into it. There will be time for all of that.

TEMPERATURE RISING

Cathryn Fox

The room was dark and smoky, with the warm tang of sex hanging heavy in the air.

With a strawberry daiquiri in hand, Delilah Morgan spun around on her vinyl-padded bar stool. Her eyes took in the Friday night crowd as they relaxed at the Hose, a local watering hole where the firefighters from Station 419 regularly gathered for a game of eight-ball.

Her salacious glance stopped to linger on three sexy firefighters working their way around the pool table, their athletic bodies, low-riding jeans, and tight backsides sending her thoughts in an erotic direction. As she took pleasure in the delicious sight before her, hot flames licked up her thighs, her skin burning hotter than molten lava.

She watched them a moment longer, and when their teasing jibes and raucous laughter drifted past her ears, the rich sound resonated through her body and pulled a shiver from deep within. Her pussy moistened with want and she squeezed her thighs together, secretly enjoying the pulsing sensations tugging at her. But there was nothing she could do to hide the telltale hardening of her nipples or the suggestive way they scraped against her light summer dress.

When the front door opened, Delilah drew a fueling breath and strove to pull herself together. Thankful for the distraction, she twisted sideways on her stool, hoping her blind date had finally arrived, but when she spotted the town's youngest fire chief darkening the doorway—a man whose reputation preceded him—awareness prowled through her bloodstream and spiked her temperature from simmer to inferno.

Looking like sex incarnate in his fire-resistant pants and suspenders, his heavy coat thrown over one broad shoulder, the man was every woman's fantasy come true. His fiery blue eyes scanned the establishment. Then, with a slow, sexy movement, he angled his head her way. When their eyes met and locked, her pussy creamed in heated response and all she could think about was how that hard body of his would feel moving over hers, how that sensuous mouth would feel on her skin, and how his rock hard cock would feel ravaging her pussy, fucking her in a way no man had ever fucked her before. She licked her suddenly dry lips, taking in his confident bad-boy attitude and the suggestive look in his eyes as they moved over her body—a look that held all kinds of erotic possibilities.

There was no question he had a raw sexuality about him, one that made Delilah ache deep in her core. But since he also had trouble written all over him, she turned away before he could see her tight nipples beneath the low-cut dress she'd purchased for this occasion—a dress, she hoped, would seduce her blind date, so she could finally fulfill a lifelong fantasy.

Even though she had her back to the fire chief, she could still *feel* him, his hot gaze on her body, as he cut across the

wide expanse of floor. She took another sip of her drink to cool
the heat zinging through her veins, but when he stepped up to
her, pressed his warm mouth against her ear, and said, "The
name's Jonah," it was all she could do not to go up in flames.
His heat reached out to her, and when she pulled his rich, spicy
scent into her lungs, everything in her gut said he was the man,
the only man, who could help extinguish the long burning fire
inside her.

But he was dangerous, she reminded herself.

Dangerous.

She sucked in air, his nearness making her breathless. "I
know who you are," she managed to get out as her pussy quivered with hunger, begging her to lay herself bare and let this
man take her to places she'd never been before.

He dropped his coat onto the counter, grabbed her stool, and
spun her around until she faced him.

When she gripped the counter, his gaze flickered over her left
hand, stopping to note the tan line on her ring finger.

"And I know who you are, *Mrs.* Morgan." Something about
the way he said *Mrs.* told her he was testing the sound of it on
his lips, savoring the sensations as it rolled off the soft blade of
his tongue.

As he invaded her space, he raked his fingers through his
dark, mussed hair and looked past her shoulder to peruse the
room. "Are you here alone?"

With her body trembling from his close proximity, she shot a
glance toward the front door. "Yes. No. I don't know."

A knowing grin pulled at his lips. "Well, which is it?" he
asked, the heat between them undeniable as he inched closer,
his warm breath doing the most delicious things to her libido.

"You're either alone or you're not." His rough voice played
down her spine like liquid fire—but before she could give him

an answer, he dropped onto the stool beside her, and in a bold move that took her by surprise, hauled her to her feet and pulled her between his thighs. As he created a delicious friction between their bodies, dark passion danced in his eyes. "I don't think he's...*coming,* sweetheart."

Delilah's skin came alive as that one suggestive word bounced around inside her head like a pinball, and with the way his cock was pressing against her pussy, only her thin cotton dress and his pants separating skin from skin. She wanted to throw caution to the wind, to indulge in a wild night with a man who clearly knew his way around a woman's body. The way his big hands curled around her hips, dipping closer and closer to the moist juncture between her legs, was a testament to his bedroom skills.

His eyes fixed on her mouth and his lips twisted in a half smile, making him look edgy, wild, and oh-so-tempting. "Want to get out of here?" he asked.

Delilah bit her lip, and her body flushed hotly. The man was the epitome of sex, sin, and seduction, and everything inside her urged her to go, to let him fulfill the fantasy that had been plaguing her dreams for years, even though she knew that after a night with him, her life would forever be altered.

"What if he shows?"

"Then it's his loss."

"But—"

"Sweetheart," he murmured, purposely putting his mouth close to her ear. "No man should ever make a woman like you wait." He inched back, and his blue eyes glistened with promise when he pitched his voice low and added, "I'd never make you wait."

Her heart began pounding, her brain racing as sexual tension arced between them. This man might be trouble with a capital

T, but was she really going to pass up the opportunity to experience his brand of lovemaking, to finally fulfill a fantasy with a sexy firefighter who would undoubtedly rock her world?

As she warmed to the idea, her body began trembling with need, eager to feel his mouth on hers, on her breasts. Deep between her legs.

Jonah seemed to know the exact moment when she made up her mind. Climbing from his stool, he grabbed his coat, slid his hand to the small of her back, and without looking back, guided her to the front door.

Once they were outside, a warm summer breeze blew her dress around her thighs, but the night air did little to cool the heat inside her.

He gestured with a nod toward the fire station across the street, and when he commanded in a soft, but firm voice, "Come with me while I put away my gear," Delilah wondered if he could read her deepest desires, if he'd somehow managed to tap into one of her scintillating fantasies.

Strides purposeful, he ushered her across the near-deserted street. Lamplight illuminated his hard body and provided her with sufficient light to see the rippling of his muscles beneath his T-shirt. As she took pleasure in his physique, he shot her a sidelong glance, his passion-imbued eyes so full of raw hunger it was all she could do to keep her legs from failing.

Delilah gulped air, her blood pressure soaring, and she briefly wondered if she was getting in way over her head.

Jonah pushed open the door to the garage and ushered her inside. When he came close, crowding her with his hard body, she exhaled slowly and decided she'd come too far to back down now. Gathering her bravado, she glanced around and a small thrill travelled the length of her spine when she spotted three fire trucks all lined up like obedient soldiers. Heat rushed through her body as she looked them over, thinking about the brave men who drove them into danger.

She ran her finger over the smooth red paint and followed Jonah to the back of the room. When the scent of fresh wax reached her nostrils, erotic images of this bad boy taking her up against the truck set a low moan rumbling in the depths of her throat.

"You okay, sweetheart?" Jonah asked, but everything in the way he looked at her told her he knew all about her secret fetish.

Unable to find her voice, she nodded and her feet stilled as she sucked in a quick, sharp breath. A firm hand closed over hers and tugged, setting her back into motion. The soft lights fell over their bodies, but she didn't miss the mischievous grin curling Jonah's lips as he wound one thumb around his suspenders.

It made her wonder what he was going to do with them.

He led her to the back of the truck, to where all the fire-fighting gear hung on hooks. The great care he took in hanging his jacket told her how thorough those deft hands of his would be with her body. As she considered that further, he unhooked his suspenders and met her glance.

"Hold these for me, would you?"

Jonah placed the stretchy suspenders in her outstretched arms, and before she even realized what he was doing, he had her hands wrapped in the straps and tied behind her back.

"Jonah," she rushed out, breathless. "What...what are you doing?"

"It's like this, *Mrs.* Morgan," he began as he backed her up and hooked the suspenders to the truck. "I've wanted you for a very long time, and now that I have you right where I want you, I don't plan on letting you go anytime soon."

Delilah tugged on the binding only to find it secure. It quickly occurred to her that this man had her captive, his to do with as he pleased. His glance moved up and down her body, a slow, leisurely inspection that had her burning from the inside out.

He ran the back of his hand along her curves, groaned deep, and wet his lips before adding, "There are so many things I want to do to you."

Oh God, there were so many things she wanted him to do to her, too. But she wasn't sure about the suspenders. No one had ever tied her up before.

Before she could give it another thought, Jonah sank to his knees. Need gathered in the pit of her stomach as he gripped her legs to widen them. Then with a move that left her head spinning and her cunt pulsing, he slid his large hands under her dress. Want burned a lazy path up her thighs as his rough palms moved upward, coming perilously close to her quivering pussy, but never quite touching. Feeling feverish with need, her skin began burning wherever he touched.

When he finally reached her damp sex, his nostrils flared and every muscle in his body tensed. A dark, tortured look came over his face. "Baby," he murmured, almost breathless, "you're not wearing any panties." His knowing glance moved over her face, assessing her. "You really *were* waiting for someone tonight, weren't you?"

She gave a sheepish smile, but knew better than to lie. If she wanted to live out this erotic fantasy, to wring every last drop of sex from this sexy encounter, then she had to be honest and tell him what she really wanted, what her body craved.

Driven by need, she jutted her hips forward. "It's just that... well...I need—"

He cut her off with a glance, widened her wet lips with his fingers, then pushed one all the way up inside her.

The hot stab of pleasure stole the breath from her lungs.

When a low, moan crawled out of her throat, he groaned out loud. "What you need, sweetheart, is *me,* inside you, because you're on fire and I'm the only man in this town who can put out these kinds of flames."

His thumb scraped over her clit and she gulped, her pussy fluttering beneath his careful ministrations. Good God, the man knew just how to touch her, knew just what she needed from him. He pumped once, twice, and she was so aroused she could feel small tremors pulling at her core. She was close, so damn close, but instead of letting her tumble over, he climbed up her body, his mouth closing over hers.

His kiss was deep, sensual, highly erotic, and the way his body was pressing against her, caging her between his chest and the truck, had to be the sexiest thing she'd ever felt.

Tongue parrying with his, she gave a tug on the straps, wanting to touch him in return, but when she found her hands immobilized, she began trembling from head to toe, a hot wave of passion singeing her blood. Maybe getting tied up turned her on more than she realized. And maybe he knew her wants and needs better than she herself did.

His deft hands went to the buttons on her dress, but instead of tediously opening them one by one, he gripped the material and pulled.

Delilah gave an excited gasp as a button clattered to the floor.

Giving her no time to catch her breath, he pulled open the dress to expose her naked body, his eyes going to her lust-swollen nipples. He wet his lips and his breath came in a low rush.

Delilah stood there for a long, agonizing minute as he inched back to take in her nakedness. Dark scalding eyes full of raw hunger flickered over her breasts. Then he leaned toward her and swiped his tongue over one hard bud before pulling it into his hot mouth.

She let loose a moan as his fiery tongue burned her flesh and sent shockwaves rocketing through her.

As she writhed against his mouth, he sucked, nibbled, nipped, and licked until she was sure she was going to come from nipple stimulation alone. She arched her back, wanting, *needing* more. "Please, Jonah," she begged. The chemistry between them was explosive.

Deserting her breasts, he dragged his tongue down her body, stopping to dip into her sensitive belly button before settling himself on his knees. His hand moved to her cunt, and he stroked her lightly before pulling her lips open to expose her pink dampness.

A low growl of longing sounded deep in his throat. "So fucking gorgeous," he murmured from between her legs.

The scent of her arousal reached her nostrils and she bucked against his mouth, desperate to feel him inside her.

He pressed a hand to her stomach to still her, then leaned forward to run his wet tongue all the way from the bottom of her pussy to the top.

Her body trembled, her skin engulfed in flames as waves of heat colored her flesh. "Yes," she cried out as she concentrated on the glorious pleasure zinging through her veins.

He pushed his face in deeper, feasting on her as he shoved one finger inside. He lightly stroked her G-spot, and her legs weakened. God, he was so skilled, so familiar with the workings of her body.

He stroked her deeper, then changed the tempo as she basked in his touch. He feathered his tongue over her pussy, stopping to press against her engorged clit, each swipe of his tongue pushing her higher and higher. Everything in the intimate way he pleasured her became her undoing, and she tugged on the straps, needing in the most desperate way to touch him in return.

As if he understood exactly what she needed, his light caresses became harder, faster, adding the right amount of pressure as he ravaged her pussy. In no time at all, soft quakes began at her core, and she panted and screamed his name. Tension grew in her body, rising in strength until it came to a peak.

"Jonah," she cried, quivering beneath his intimate touch as her sex clenched around his finger, her hot liquid searing his mouth.

He stayed between her legs, lavishing her cunt with little devilish strokes, drawing out her pleasure until she rode out every last wave.

When her body stopped spasming, he climbed to his feet, and the intensity in his eyes was as frightening as it was exciting. "I need to be inside you, sweetheart."

She could tell he was losing it and was desperately trying to maintain some kind of control. But she didn't want him in control. She wanted him as crazed as she was. Feeling almost frantic she said, "I want you to fuck me, Jonah."

Her words pulled the reaction she was hoping for. His glance, a turbulent mixture of fire and heat as they met hers, searched her face.

"I want it hard," she added.

His nostrils flared and with one quick thrust he freed her bound hands. After kicking his pants and shorts off, he lifted her off her feet and ordered in a rough voice, "Put your legs around me."

When she obliged, he slammed her back against the truck, and drove his cock into her so hard and so deep she thought she'd died and gone to heaven.

She squirmed and writhed and clawed at his back as he

buried his mouth into the deep hollow of her neck. He called out her name and a riot of emotions moved through her as he bucked forward, filling her in a way no man ever had before.

"Yes," she cried out. "More."

Keeping one hand around her waist, he balanced the other on the truck beside her head, and pushed deeper, driving her impossibly higher, like he was laying claim to her. Branding her as his.

She bucked forward to meet each thrust, and dug her nails into his back. She could feel his muscles tighten as he fucked her the way she needed to be fucked. Her heart picked up tempo as he continued to pound into her—hot, hard strokes that had her body trembling, her cunt rippling with the approach of another powerful orgasm.

The second she came apart in his arms and her hot cream dripped over his cock, he adjusted his body for deeper thrusts.

Delilah rocked against him, savoring the glorious feel of him inside her, taking her to places she knew only he could take her. His fingers burrowed into her hair, and when she felt his impressive girth tighten and thicken inside her, she murmured, "That's it, Jonah. Come inside me."

With that he threw his head back, bucked forward once more, then came with a growl, jettisoning his seed high inside her. They stayed like that for a long time, both trying to regulate their breathing.

A moment later, once they finally found their breath, he pressed his lips to her quivering flesh and moaned against her neck. "So good. So fucking good." He inched back, and let her legs slide to the floor. He smiled down at her and brushed her damp hair from her forehead.

A deep sense of satisfaction rolled through her—but despite a wild night of sex, she suspected that when it came to this sexy bad boy, nothing could ever assuage the deep ache in her core. Because the truth was she wanted him again.

Without speaking he led her to the shower area, and a warm comfortable silence fell over them as they washed each other's bodies. Once complete, he helped her back into her torn dress.

He pulled her close, but she noticed the time on the station clock when he brushed his thumb over her kiss-swollen lips. "I'd better get going," she murmured.

"I'll take you home."

"It's just around the corner."

"Then I'll take you just around the corner," he insisted, and there was something so sexy in his take-charge attitude that her pussy moistened for him all over again.

He grabbed his coat off the hook to drape it over her shoulders. His familiar scent teased her senses, and when he slipped his hand around her waist to lead her outside, she couldn't help but think his touch was more emotional than physical.

Less than ten minutes later, he led her up the stairs to her condo. She turned to him; she wasn't quite ready for sleep. "Nightcap?" she asked. When he nodded, she opened her door, and moved inside.

Without speaking, Jonah followed her in and glanced around the cozy home.

"I need to slip into something more comfortable." When their eyes met in understanding, she handed him back his jacket. She pointed toward the liquor cabinet. "Why don't you go make those nightcaps. I'll join you in a minute."

With that she slipped down the hall. She could hear him remove his boots and pad softly across the hardwood floor.

She hurried to her dresser, but as she pulled open the drawer her glance landed on her wedding photo. An invisible fist squeezed her heart as she picked it up. Without conscious thought, she stroked a finger over the handsome groom standing beside her, looking at her with pure love in his eyes.

Her glance fell to the date engraved in the silver frame, a reminder that the picture was taken exactly three years ago.

Today was her anniversary.

A noise at the door pulled her focus, and she glanced up to see Jonah standing there, two glasses of wine in his hand.

"Everything okay?"

She lowered the picture quickly and grabbed a silk nightgown from her dresser. "Yes, I was just..."

He stepped up to her until his chest was pressed against her back. "You were just what?"

"I was just thinking about three years ago today."

Jonah set the drinks down and took her nightgown from her hands. He tossed it on the dresser and said, "You don't need this." Then he proceeded to slip her torn dress from her shoulders. Once he had her stripped bare, he carried her to her bed, pulled back the sheets, and placed her inside.

He stared down at her for a long moment, taking in her nakedness before pulling something out of his front pocket. With one hand balled into a fist, he made short work of his clothes and climbed in beside her. He pulled her close and as he kissed her mouth, he murmured, "I want to make love to you again, *Mrs.* Morgan."

Love swelled inside her heart for all the things this man did for her, for all the fantasies he was willing to fulfill. "I want to make love to you too, Jonah. Or should I say *Mr.* Morgan?"

He captured her left hand and opened his palm to reveal her wedding band. "I believe this belongs to you." He slipped it on her finger, and his sexy grin turned her inside out when he dropped a soft kiss onto her mouth and said, "Happy anniversary, baby."

She pulled him to her and opened her arms and her body to him, knowing she was the luckiest woman in the world. No man could make her heart race quite like Jonah could, and she was looking forward to spending a lifetime fulfilling fantasies with a heroic man who knew just how to make her temperature rise.

UNEXPECTED DETOUR

Ily Goyanes

José looked down at his bare chest and admired the soot stains. He'd been jogging by one of the many *cafeterias* in downtown San Juan, noticed smoke billowing from the building up into the azure sky, and had run inside to see if he could help.

Out for his morning run, he'd run into the burning building wearing only basketball shorts and his well-worn running shoes—not exactly regulation—but that hadn't stopped him. His captain would have his ass on Monday, at least on paper, but the write-up in his personnel file wouldn't reveal the pride and admiration his brothers-in-arms would demonstrate behind closed doors.

He felt a light touch on his bicep and looked down to see the young lady he'd pulled out of the *cafeteria* and away from the fire. Like many Puerto Rican women, she had large brown eyes and thick, dark hair. She smiled tentatively, but squeezed his muscular arm affectionately.

"*Gracias,*" she said. "*Me salvaste la vida.*"

José turned towards her, his six-three frame towering over her barely-over-five-foot body. *"De nada.* I was just doing my job." She was unusually beautiful, José noticed, wishing that his last heartache hadn't diminished his spirit to the point where he couldn't ask a woman out on a date without feeling as if he would have a panic attack. He ran into burning buildings for a living and went cliff diving for fun, but the thought of being hurt again terrified him.

Her eyes opened wide when she realized that he spoke English—not everyone on the island did. She clapped her hands excitedly. "Oh! You are a fireman?" she asked, speaking English with a cute sing-song quality he found endearing.

José nodded. "Ten years now, ma'am. I joined the academy right out of high school."

"My name is Isabella. It is a pleasure to meet you."

José noted the curvy body under her soot-covered sundress. Even through the loose cotton, there was no mistaking her Latin curves. He put his hand out. "I'm José, and the pleasure is all mine." And it was, he thought. Her golden skin and thick wavy hair were the stuff his dreams were made of.

She winked at him then, and he felt a surge of adrenaline course through his body. The men at the firehouse called that feeling a "rescue high." But José felt as if the heat taking over his body on this particular occasion had more to do with the woman he'd rescued than with the rescue itself.

When their hands met, he could tell she was feeling it too.

Isabella blushed and looked down. When she looked up again, there was a mischievous gleam in her eyes. "Can I take you home?" she asked, quickly adding, "I mean, can I give you a ride home? You saved my life, it's the least I can do." She looked back at the *cafeteria*, and then back at him. "I'm pretty sure I'll be getting the day off."

José chuckled, and before he knew what he was doing, he put his arm around her protectively. Being saved was even more intense than saving someone. He knew she was experiencing an altered state of consciousness. Almost dying had this eerie way of making you feel more alive.

He heard sirens approaching and felt a sudden and irrational worry. He didn't want this to be the last time he saw Isabella. In fact, he wanted more than anything to let her "take him home." Putting aside his cultivated caution with the opposite sex, he blurted out, "I appreciate the offer, but why don't we stop by your place so you can pick up a change of clothes? Then you can give me a ride home, take a shower, and change while I fix us something to eat."

She looked up at him again, her warm, tan hand caressing his bare arm. "You cook, too?" she asked, winking again.

José nodded. "Not that well, but I do make a mean *pan con churrasco* and *papas fritas.*"

Isabella smiled. "A steak sandwich with fries happens to be my favorite meal."

A few seconds later, they were climbing into her jeep. Isabella put on some Robbie Williams and his sultry voice filled their heads. As Isabella drove, José looked out at the green mountains. He'd been born to do this—save people. Although he'd been born in Puerto Rico, he'd grown up in the States as an Army brat. His father had pushed him to join too, but José knew he wanted to serve his people at home—not in some godforsaken desert. As a firefighter, he witnessed the results of his heroic efforts firsthand.

After his first fire, when he'd scooped a six-month-old girl from her crib seconds before it went up in flames, there was no turning back. Esmeralda, now ten years old, still emailed him and referred to him as *padrino,* godfather.

* * *

Isabella couldn't help but sneak looks at José as she drove. He seemed lost in thought—Robbie Williams could do that. He had a serene look on his handsome face. She took in his long eyelashes, his thick, tousled hair, his chiseled brow and sensuous lips, and couldn't stop herself from imaging how he would look without the basketball shorts and running shoes. She pictured his tall, muscular body naked, about to enter her...

Just as the image entered her mind, José turned to look at her. She immediately glanced back at the road, staring straight ahead and gripping the wheel as if her life depended on it.

José smiled. "Are you a native?" he asked.

He felt comfortable around her, easy, the way he used to feel around women before the divorce.

She nodded. "Yes. I've never even been off the island. I work at the *cafeteria* while I go to school."

"What are you studying?"

"I want to be a pediatric nurse. I love babies," she said shyly.

José smiled and placed his large hand on her thigh. "I bet they love you too."

Isabella felt a rapid heat spread through her thighs, up over her mound, and into her belly. It was as if all her nerve endings were on fire—she felt so physical, so engaged, so *alive*. She took his hand and placed it between her legs, inviting him to feel the heat and moisture he had created.

José's hand was directly on the crotch of her moist cotton panties. His prick hardened instantly and he applied pressure to her swollen pussy, his fingers rubbing her swollen lips.

The jeep veered off the road as Isabella drove into the nearest village, making the turn for El Yunque, the island's national rainforest. As she drove up the winding road that led to the top of the mountains, José continued to caress her increasingly wet cunt.

She pulled haphazardly onto the side of the road and they both dismounted without saying a word. Holding hands, they meandered through the trees until they were at least twenty feet from the road, surrounded by overgrown foliage and the inimitable chirping of *coquis,* the national frog.

She put her arms around José's neck and looked deep into his dark eyes. *"Te necesito,"* she said huskily.

José grabbed her and pulled her tightly against him, his hard cock pushing against her flat belly. "I need you too," he growled before pressing his lips down on hers.

Their mouths opened and their tongues explored. The heat they felt was primal. Surrounded by the sounds of the rainforest, San Juan seemed to exist on another plane. There was no place here for courtship, rules, etiquette. Their lust was overwhelming, and its call had to be answered immediately.

José slipped her sundress off as she pulled down his shorts. He quickly kicked off his running shoes and dropped to his knees in front of Isabella. First, he undid her *sandalias,* and then he pulled down her pink cotton panties.

Isabella let out a loud moan as José pressed his face tightly against her wet pussy and inhaled her scent. He parted her lips with his strong fingers and traced her slit with his warm, wet tongue.

"I need you," she moaned, grabbing onto his thick black hair. "I need you *now.*"

José stood up and lifted her slight body over his shoulder, carrying her to a nearby tree. After setting her down on a pile of leaves, he knelt between her legs and looked up at her pretty face. "And you will have me," he said, his voice shaky. "But I need to taste you first."

Isabella opened her legs wide as José's face neared her sweet spot. Her mind, body, and soul cried out in unison as soon as his thick tongue landed on her clit. She pulled at his hair as he lapped up her juices, crying out his name.

José had never tasted anything as sweet as Isabella's beautiful, shaved cunt. He sucked on it greedily, pushing two fingers inside of her and working her tight hole. His cock was over nine inches when hard, and he wanted to make sure she was ready for it.

Isabella thrashed about on the leaves, her pussy clenching and unclenching as she came for José. Her fingernails left bright, red marks on his neck and shoulders as she clawed at his flesh, trying to get him to come up for air.

"Please," she whimpered, unable to wait for his cock any longer.

José knew she was ready. He moved away from her intoxicating scent and lay on top of her, their bodies producing a heat that rivaled any Puerto Rican summer night.

Isabella wrapped her legs around his back, pulling him even tighter against her. "*Te necesito,*" she said again, tracing his jawline, chin, and lips with her tongue. "I need you inside me. Fill me. Take me right here, right now."

José's prick was more than ready, and had been since she had taken his hand in the car and placed it between her caramel-colored thighs. Now he pushed his massive cock head against her tight hole, immersing the first few inches of his swollen meat inside her.

Isabella groaned and pulled him in deeper. "All of it. Please. *Por favor, José.* I need it."

Her words lit a fire inside him, and he pushed his dick the rest of the way in. They both let out a loud groan as he filled her wet pussy.

"*Sí! Sí!*" Isabella cried, her hands clutching his firm ass, pulling him in as much as she could.

"Ay, Isabella," he groaned, her tight, warm cunt like heaven around his prick. He moved slowly, with smooth strokes, taking his time. They kissed like beasts, biting, sucking, and chewing each other's tongues and lips, hungry and feral.

"You feel so good," he groaned next to her ear, his hot breath sending shivers throughout her body.

Isabella looked up at him and slowly rotated her hips, working his cock. "So do you. I love the way you fill me. No man has ever gone as deep or made me stretch as wide."

They locked eyes as he continued to move inside her. They fucked in silence for several minutes, his strokes slowly gaining speed. "*Ay, ay, ay,*" Isabella moaned. "*Dios mío! Sí! Por favor, no pares,*" she said—*oh God, please don't stop.*

"I don't intend to, *chiquita,*" he said, pushing deeper. "At least not until we're both satisfied."

"*Papi,*" she moaned. "Please. I want you to fill me up. Shoot your seed inside me. Fill me with your come."

José had to stop for a second because he almost came after hearing those words. He regained control of himself and began to pump his cock fast and deep into her eager hole. "Is that what you want, *mami?*" he asked, looking so deep into her eyes that Isabella felt as if he could actually see inside of her. "You want my come inside you? Filling you? *Marking* you?"

Isabella let out an animal-like growl as her clit exploded into a half dozen orgasms. Her body trembled underneath his, and José shoved his fat dick deep into her, holding it steady inside her as she shook. "Yes! Yes! Yes! Please, José! *Hechame la, llename,*" she cried. *Shoot your load inside me, fill me up!*

José could no longer restrain himself. He held her hips down against the leaves as his cock head erupted, shooting a hot stream of salty come inside of Isabella's wet cunt. They held each other, their bodies still shaking and spent for several minutes, indulging in long, slow kisses, savoring each other's mouths.

José pulled away for a moment and looked at Isabella's beautiful face. "I guess now we're even," he said seriously. She stared at him, confused. *"¿Por qué dices eso, José?"* she asked.

"I say that because it's true," he replied, kissing her neck, cheeks, and chin. "First I saved your life, and then you saved mine."

RESCUE ME

Maggie Wells

The pounding started just as Addi Mason rinsed the conditioner from her hair. Too tired to deal with Mr. Grabowski's incessant complaining about the height of her grass, she groaned and dunked her head back under the spray. This was America, damn it. If she wanted to let her lawn grow over the two inches her nosy neighbor deemed optimum, it was her business, not his.

Another round of pounding echoed through the empty house, and she yanked open the shower curtain, glaring at the bathroom door. He even measured it! The man actually took a ruler and measured individual blades of grass. He claimed they were over five inches long but she wasn't about to double-check him. Hell, five inches wasn't enough to get any woman excited.

She switched off the water, yanked a towel from the bar, and wrapped it around her dripping body as she climbed from the tub. The wood floors were cool as she stomped through her bedroom, ramping up to give the old man a piece of her mind.

The sound of men shouting carried through the door, slowing her footsteps at the end of the hall. Had Mr. Grabowski formed some kind of posse to bring her to lawn care justice? She almost ran back to the shower, but another round of rapping steeled her resolve. Knotting the bath sheet between her breasts, she marched forward to meet the enemy head-on, but drew up short when a sharp crack split the air.

Her front door exploded.

One second it was intact; the next, shards of shrapnel from the wood frame were showering the rug and pinging off the walls.

Addi screeched, instinctively raising her arms to shield her face. The hulking figure of a man filled the open doorway. She had barely a moment to register the vision of a firefighter in full gear before he lunged through the door, barreling straight for her.

She sucked in a sharp breath and the knot unraveled. Damp terry cloth hit the floor in a heap at her feet, and his hard shoulder pressed into her stomach.

He lifted her off the ground and tossed her over his back as if she were no more than a curl of ash. A cool draft wafted across her bare ass. The rough, fire-retardant fabric of his coat abraded her nipples. His helmet crashed to the floor as he whirled. Peering under his arm, she yelped when she caught a glimpse of two more uniformed men in the open doorway.

"Hansen! Hansen, goddamn it! We've got the wrong house!" one shouted.

"We're supposed to be going to four-forty-four, not four-oh-fo—oh shit." The other man tipped his helmet back, revealing eyes as big as dinner plates.

The two men froze for a second then sprang into fast forward mode. "Hansen, come on. Wrong house. No fire here." They scurried across her scraggly lawn to the waiting truck.

Addi blinked in confusion as her feet touched down again. Gloved hands grasped her upper arms, making sure she was steady on her feet before casting about in a wild circle. The firefighter spotted her towel laying discarded on the floor and snatched it up, holding the sodden bath sheet out to her as if he were giving her a precious gift.

"Sorry." The apology came in a rush of breath. Then his eyes widened in astonishment. "Addison?"

She jerked the towel from his hands and pressed it to her chest, praying she'd unfurled enough to cover the pertinent parts. Struggling to wrap her mind around the fact that her hoo-hah had just been on display for all the neighbors to see, she shook her head to clear the haze. Her assailant knew her, but she was at a loss. He was tall. And blond. And familiar in a gut-twistingly handsome way. Like a movie star. But in her foyer.

"I'm so sorry," he said as he backed up a step.

Her hero came equipped with a raspy rumble of a voice that didn't quite match his angel-kissed face, but proved sexy enough to make her want to drop her towel again. She thought about releasing it for a full second—then she remembered that somebody's house was on fire.

"Four-forty-four. That's Mrs. Wilkins," she murmured.

The information seemed to snap him from his daze. "Shit!" He scooped his helmet from the floor and clomped his way to the front door. "I have to go."

Clutching damp terrycloth, she inched toward her decimated door. Cool air rippled her skin, and her brain finally made the connection. His name sprang to her lips as he took off at a sprint. "Trey!"

Trey Hansen, once Oakdale High's resident heartthrob, the bad boy smart girls like Addison avoided like the plague and dreamed about every night. The girls in French Club called him "Trés Handsome" and the nickname was dead on. He was the one she'd daydreamed would ask her to prom.

She would have turned him down, of course. She and Mike Mason had been a couple since Algebra I, but it would have been great to be asked by Trey. Not that he ever noticed her. He was the kind of guy who never gave her a second glance.

"Sorry about the door!" His shout carried over the dull roar of the engine. "I'll come back!"

She stared out into the waning daylight, watching as he grabbed a rail on the back of the fire truck and swung himself onto the slow-moving vehicle. The truck surged ahead. When the sound of the engine faded, the rustle of shrubbery caught her attention.

Addi tore her gaze from the swirl of red lights, slowly becoming aware of the water dripping from her hair, the painful prickle of splintered wood under her bare feet, and the stunned gaze of her elderly neighbor. It took three blinks before her brain engaged. She tightened her hold on the towel, tipped her chin up a notch, and leveled Mr. Grabowski with an unflinching stare.

"Those kids need to stay off my lawn," she announced, then turned her back on the shocked septuagenarian.

The semi-useless doorknob rattled in her hand. She closed the door, wincing when the ruptured frame kept the latch from engaging. Blowing out a breath, she leaned against the cool wood and breathed deep. She knew she should be humiliated, or at least vaguely embarrassed, but she wasn't. The only thing she felt was hot. And at the moment, she reveled in the heat. It beat the crap out of feeling empty and numb all the time.

Pressing the towel to her breasts, she sighed. The memory of that rough coat tweaking her nipples, and Trey Hansen's warm hand on the back of her thigh, would be prime fodder for the fantasies that got her through long, lonely nights. The image of his gorgeous face coupled with that sexy, husky voice made her blood sing for the first time in…forever. This one teeny-tiny blip in an otherwise dull life would keep her vibrator humming for months, if not years. The man had tossed her without regard for any perceived delicacy, and she damn well liked it. A lot.

The thought unleashed a torrent of guilt and shame. "Please let Mrs. Wilkins be okay." Her prayer came on a rush of breath, but it was Trey Hansen's parting shot that left her reeling.

"He's coming back."

She pushed from the door, her feet slapping hardwood as she dashed down the hall to her bedroom. The towel fell to the floor the moment she crossed the threshold. Hurtling herself into the walk-in closet, she grabbed the first thing that came to hand—a leopard print silk robe she'd found on clearance just before Mike died.

She'd never had a chance to wear it. Two days after she'd made the purchase, a head-on collision had robbed her of her high-school sweetheart and what seemed like her last opportunity for seduction. Until now. For the first time since the day she'd snagged the robe from the sale rack, a spark of life flared inside her.

The slippery fabric tickled her thighs. Cinching the belt tight, she made a beeline to the bathroom on a quest for her blow drier and a tube of tinted moisturizer. It seemed un-neighborly to hope Mrs. Wilkins' house was engulfed in flames long enough to allow for a complete makeover.

Trey cooled his jets on the back of the truck while Lieutenant Dolinski and a couple other guys stayed in the house to calm Mrs. Wilkins. The small kitchen fire was out before they arrived. What was left behind was minimal damage, compounded by the mess caused by the fire extinguisher. Before they left, the firefighters would probably make a few calls to set repairs in motion. That was the way things worked around here—neighbors watching out for neighbors, firemen coming to the rescue.

The possibility of rescuing a beautiful naked woman was a strong motivator in any firefighter's training, but he'd never believed it might come true. His gaze drifted in the direction of Addison's house. Of course, the only thing he'd saved that particular damsel in distress from was a hot shower.

Fires were rare occurrences in a town the size of St. Joe. They spent most of their time investigating potential gas leaks and teaching second graders to stop, drop, and roll. That is, when they weren't pulling cats from trees. That's why he climbed into his turnout gear as excited as a teenager anxious for his first handful of tit when the alarm bell rang. Nothing was going to stop him from fighting that fire. Not a door, or a lock, or a sopping-wet naked woman running smack into his arms.

"Shit."

Addison Jacobs was one of the prettiest girls he'd ever seen. Pretty and smart and worlds above a guy whose dad worked as the school janitor when he wasn't too drunk to push a mop. She'd married Mike Mason right after graduation, and the two of them had settled down to the perfect small-town life. Perfect—until Mike bought it in a car wreck. Not that her change in marital status gave him half a shot. She was a widow, and, if possible, even more untouchable than ever. Now, thanks to him, she was also a woman living alone with a busted front door.

He huffed a sigh and jumped down, stomping to the side of the truck and coming to a halt just below the driver's window. Stanley Tarklington stared down at him with a mixture of amusement and pity.

Hooking a thumb over his shoulder, Trey muttered, "Gotta

see a lady about a door." He pulled his helmet from his head and shrugged out of his jacket. "Give my gear a ride?"

The older man took the bulky equipment he passed through the window and nodded. "I'm making spaghetti tonight. I'm not keeping it warm for you."

Trey snickered and raised one hand in acknowledgement as he trudged down the sidewalk. His steps slowed to a plod when he reached her block. She had the shaggiest lawn around. He couldn't help but wonder if its owner would forgo suing the department in exchange for a trim. He smiled as the memory of warm, wiggling woman brought a different kind of trim to mind.

His heart rate dropped, slowing to a dull thud as he raised his hand to knock. The door swung open the second his knuckles touched wood. He scowled at the useless latch and shook his head.

"Hello?" Resigned, he barged into her home for the second time. "Addison? It's Trey Hansen," he called, craning his neck to peer down the short hall.

"Oh!"

He whirled toward her gasp and nearly swallowed his tongue when he spotted her hovering in the doorway opposite the narrow hall. She wore some kind of animal print robe—if that flimsy excuse for fabric could be called a robe. It was short, and silky, and barely covered the parts he'd put on display earlier.

"Hey, Trey." She tugged at the hem of the robe, but her efforts were in vain. The scant fabric barely grazed mid-thigh.

Now that he got a good look at her, he couldn't help being a little bitter about the fact he'd done all the work while the other guys got to appreciate the view. Thick red hair curved just under her chin and a pair of big brown eyes delivered a punch that sent him reeling. He bobbed a slow nod. "Addi."

She rubbed the top of one foot with the sole of the other then fussed with the tie at her waist. "You came back."

"I said I would." To put her at ease, he flashed a sheepish smile. "Seems I had a little disagreement with your door over where the fire might be." His smile faded into a wince. "I'm really sorry about this," he murmured, surveying the damage. "I got a little... No one answered, and I might have been a bit over the top." Her eyebrows rose and he tried to mask the little white lie he was about to tell with a friendly smile. "Sorry about, uh, grabbing you."

"It's okay."

Her voice was deeper than he remembered. Rich, velvety, and so husky it was almost obscene. He cleared the boulder from his throat. "I came by to secure your door for the night. I'd be happy to come back when I'm off duty tomorrow to take care of the repair."

"You'd do that?"

He raised one shoulder. "I'm the one who kicked it." His suspender slipped and he yanked the strap back into place, shifting his weight. "I'm, uh...I was sorry to hear about Mike."

She nodded, but the warm glow faded from her eyes. "Thank you." She held the lapels of the robe closed at the base of her throat. "I have a toolkit in the kitchen. Maybe you can take a look and see if it has what you need."

Trey followed her into the sunshine-yellow room. Ruffled curtains framed the window above the sink. The décor reflected its owner: unflinchingly feminine and gut-wrenchingly inviting. The slinky robe crept up the backs of her thighs, exposing the sweet curve of her ass when she bent to peer into a cabinet.

She straightened, clutching the toolkit to her chest. "I appreciate your help."

Her voice was soft and sounded sincere, but the stubborn set of her chin told him she didn't appreciate his offer one bit. He took one step closer, accepting the plastic box she thrust at him.

"You know, you can tell me to piss off if you want." She inhaled sharply and he chanced a cautious smile. "But I would really like to stay and fix the door so I can sleep tonight. I love sleeping."

"I'm not helpless."

He met those big brown eyes directly and waited for her to continue.

"I've been handling things on my own for a long time now."

He smiled. "Gotcha. You're tough as stale beef jerky."

Her eyes widened, then danced. She let loose a breathy laugh and turned toward the fridge, shaking her head in dismay. "I'm sorry. I didn't mean to snap at you. It's been a stressful night."

"What with getting your door kicked in and being hoisted up and carried around stark naked?"

"Among other things," she replied, a sly smirk accompanying her cryptic response. She pulled two beers from the fridge and offered one to him, steadfastly ignoring his excuses about being on duty. Smart woman.

He returned her smile and reached for both longnecks, twisting off the caps before handing one back to her. She toasted him with the bottle, and the front of her robe gaped just enough to expose a hint of breast. "To you, Firefighter Handsome."

He chuckled then rolled his eyes at the old nickname. She ran her tongue across her lower lip, meeting his gaze directly. The laugh died in his parched throat. His blood flow shifted to parts further south. He blinked to clear the haze of lust from his vision.

"Are you flirting with me, Mrs. Mas—" he stumbled to a stop when she flinched.

"Addi," she corrected in a sultry hush. She pushed away from the counter and stepped into his space. Delicate silk snagged on the nubby nylon of his suspender. Her breasts grazed his chest. He took two quick steps back, putting the tiny dinette table between them.

A rosy blush tinted her cheeks. "I'm sorry. I didn't mean to embarrass you." She wet her lips, then shook her head. "Ignore me," she whispered in a rush.

"Not a chance. And I'm not embarrassed."

Lifting her chin, she gave him a tight smile. "Don't worry about the door. I can fix it myself."

Annoyed by her easy dismissal, he rushed headlong into the fire. She jerked when he kicked a chair aside in his haste to get to her but he didn't care. She opened her mouth to speak, and he covered it with his. He slipped one hand under her robe and his palm formed to the curve of her lush, ripe ass as if she were made for him.

Addi moaned when the tip of his tongue traced the seam of her lips. The moment they parted he swept in, tasting the heady tang of hops on her tongue. He flexed his knees and lifted her up, groaning into her mouth as she wound her arms around his neck and held on. He cleared the table with one sweep of his arm.

She broke the kiss, gasping as he parted her robe. "Oh God, no one has touched me in so long. Not like you did earlier—like I wouldn't shatter into a million pieces." Arching her back, she thrust her chin at the ceiling, offering herself up to him. "I can take it. Touch me. Please touch me."

He did as she asked, filling his palms with her breasts and teasing her nipples with the pads of his thumbs. The rosy tips puckered and reached for him, begging for more. He kissed her again, his tongue tangling with hers. He pinched the hardened points and her teeth sank into his lower lip. Blood pooled in his mouth and rushed to his dick.

"Christ."

The word bounced off her skin—half-prayer, half-curse. He ground against her, trying desperately to get closer, but thwarted by thick layers of protective clothing. Swearing under his breath, he shrugged out of his suspenders and tore at the fastenings on his bunker pants.

She pressed her palms to his cheeks, stroking his temples and pulling him down. Her mouth met his once more and the soft warmth of her lips was too much to resist.

Her hands burrowed under his T-shirt, and he took the kiss deeper. Nimble fingers found the button at the waistband of the fatigues he wore under his gear. She laughed when it gave way, a triumphant exhalation that consumed the precious oxygen in his lungs.

He shoved the protective gear down to his knees then plunged his hands into her hair, tipping her head back. Her throaty purr shot straight to his groin.

One hand braced on the table, he pressed his lips to the pulse below her ear and tried to slow the rasp of his breath, seeking refuge from the heat bubbling inside him. "Addi—"

"Don't think," she panted. Her palms ruffled the hair on his stomach as she bunched the thin cotton of his T-shirt under his arms. She raked her thumbnail over his nipple and he groaned long and loud. "Touch me. Want me. I just need you to want me. I want you to rescue me."

"I want you." His breathing grew ragged. "I want you so bad it hurts."

"Do you?"

"Jesus, can't you tell?"

He pressed his crotch to the slick fabric covering her pussy, pinning her to the table with the evidence. He ducked his head and buried his face in her neck, inhaling the fresh scent of soap and fruity shampoo. Drawing her earlobe into his mouth, he sucked lightly before letting his teeth sink into the tender flesh. Her hands ran wild over his back, stoking the fire smoldering inside him with each stroke.

Summoning his strength, he lifted his body from hers, stretching to his full height. Her lips were as red as ripe berries, swollen from his kisses. A pale pink burn from his beard stubble blushed the pearly skin of her throat. The faint imprint of tooth marks shadowed her delicate ear. His chest heaved as he stared into her eyes, trying to find the self-control to be chivalrous but all the while praying she wouldn't want him to be.

She shook her head in answer to his unspoken question. "I don't want to stop. Don't stop."

The rasp of his zipper sent a shudder down his spine. She dragged his underwear down with his pants and wrapped cool fingers around his stiff dick. She drew one knee up and he cradled the supple skin of her thigh, taking one last shot at sanity. "Bedroom?" he rasped.

Addi arched her back and tugged at the sash of her robe, letting the slick fabric fall open. "Here. Now."

She was satin skin poured over pooled silk, hot and sweet and his for the taking. He yanked her to the edge of the table, leaving no room for doubt.

Her eyes flew open and he met her stunned gaze with a wicked smile. "Here. Now."

He backed the words with action, pressing the head of his cock to her pussy and rocking against her. Splayed on the table, she stared up at him, her hair a bank of dark flames behind her head, and her pale skin shining with a fine layer of sweat. Her dusky nipples were furled tight. Her cunt was hot and slick with desire.

She stared up at him, her dark eyes fathomless and knowing.

"Fuck me," she whispered. "Fuck me so hard I'll ache for days. I won't break, I swear."

"I know."

He snagged a lock of cinnamon hair with his forefinger and dragged it from her damp lips before claiming them. She rose to meet him, her kiss sweet and tender. Her breath came in tiny puffs as he thrust into her, driving his dick into that hot, tight channel hard enough to move the table.

Addi cried out, her fingernails biting into his biceps as he withdrew, gathering steam for another assault. She stared up at him, her eyes wide and more than a little wild. "Again."

He complied, surging into her with enough force to lose his balance. He stumbled, scooting the table another six inches and crushing her when he fell.

And she laughed.

The joyful sound grabbed his heart and squeezed hard. Her entire body shook, sending bolts of pleasure through his frayed nerve endings and setting his blood to simmer. She held on tight, wrapping her legs around his torso and tilting her hips up to meet him. Her lips grazed his neck and jaw before landing on his ear. "You okay?"

He couldn't hold back a chuckle of his own. His shoulders slumped even as his dick strained inside her. "I'm so much better in bed," he muttered. He peered down at her. "Next time, we're doing this in a bed."

Her eyebrows arched eloquently. "Next time?"

He met her probing stare with a blank expression. "You weren't just thinking you'd use me for sex and carpentry, were you?"

She snorted. "You aren't just sleeping with me to keep me from filing a complaint about the damage to my front door, are you?"

He grinned and shook his head. "No, ma'am. Of course not." His dick jerked inside her, and he smirked as she circled her hips in response to his call to action. "I'm sleeping with you because I used to dream about you."

"You did?"

The breathy wonder in her tone spoke volumes. "I wanted you." He drove his point home with a series of hard, hot thrusts. "Wanted to be inside you." She moaned, throwing fuel on the fire his admission ignited. Her pussy clenched around him and he ground his teeth, trying to hold on long enough to get her there first. "I shoulda kicked your locker door in."

Her breathless laugh morphed into a gasp. He shifted slightly, rising onto his toes and surging into her wet heat from above, stroking her clit as he plunged into her again and again. The air crackled, splintering all around them. The earth tilted off its axis as her muscles spasmed, milking the dregs of restraint from his body. She cried out and his blood roared in his ears as he shot off like a roman candle, driving into her sweet, tight pussy until he collapsed on top of her, gasping for air.

He slid back down to earth far faster than anticipated, twisting at the last second to cushion her fall. The cold tile floor knocked what little wind he had left from his lungs. He blinked at the shattered leg on the dinette table in astonishment. "Holy crap."

Addi's lashes fluttered as she craned her neck, following his gaze. He felt the laugh bubbling up inside her before it erupted. She gaped at him, her chest heaving with shock and exertion. "Are you trying to trash the whole place?"

"Holy crap," he repeated, unable to restrain a chuckle. Wrapping his arms around her, he hugged her hard and shook his head. "You said you wouldn't break, but I should have asked about the table."

Her entire body trembled with laughter, sending a fresh round of aftershocks straight to his groin. Regret tinged his voice. "I have to go back to work, and I didn't even get your door fixed."

She snuggled into the crook of his neck. "I can handle it."

He brushed her hair from her face and smiled at the ceiling. "Oh, I know you can, but tonight you'll stay at my place." She lifted her head to look at him, and he raised his eyebrows in unspoken challenge. "When I get home in the morning, we'll do our best to break my bed. That way, we can call it even. Deal?"

A sly smile tipped her lips. "Deal."

CHASING FIRE

Elle James

C hance Muldoon checked his gear one more time as he stood
beside the plane's open door, wind blasting his face, the
acrid scent of smoke already burning his nostrils. Ahead of them,
in the distance, red flames shot high as fire lit the evening sky to
the west. Towering stands of Ponderosa pines, already ravaged
by ravenous pine beetles, lit up like torches. A hot summer wind
charged across the mountains like a freight train, fanning the
flames, sending flames higher, climbing the hills, consuming all
which lay before it at a breathtaking pace.

Adrenaline shot through Chance's veins as he prepared to
jump in front of the fast-moving line of fiery death. This was his
world, his job, his life as a smoke jumper.

"Ready?" the most experienced spotter, also their strike
team leader, called out.

Six other men, all wearing similar jumpsuits, harnessed into
parachutes and lined up behind Chance, who nodded, prepared
to jump on command.

The chief pointed at a break between the trees, where what looked like a slim thread of silver shone up through the gathering smoke. "Anchor point is between that stream and the rock escarpment," he shouted over the roar of the engines. "We'll create our own fireline and then backburn to consume the fuel ahead of the storm."

Chance gave him another nod, patted his chute, and checked the big harness on the paracargo box full of the tools and equipment they would need for the fight. The jumper's job was to jump ahead of the fire and create a break in the fire's path to rob it of the fuel it needed to continue its march across thousands of acres of forest. An entire community of more than a hundred homes stood in the path of the raging inferno. If they didn't stop it first, the homes would be nothing more than tinder, burnt to a crisp, when the beast was done with them. Any livestock or unfortunate animals left behind would be killed, either burned to death or succumbing to smoke inhalation.

The strike team leader shouted. "Go!"

A team of paracargo handlers shoved the box out the door. The static line jerked and the paracargo chute opened, lifting it up and away from the aircraft.

When the spotter called out "Go!" again, Chance didn't think, didn't hesitate. As the first man standing at the door, he jumped. As soon as he cleared the fuselage, the static line triggered the release of his parachute and it unfurled, jerking him upward.

The plane flew on, dropping its load of jumpers two at a time, chutes bursting open like popcorn in the sky.

Once they were out of the plane, the engine noise faded, the only sound filling the sky the roar of the fire storming across the mountains, an angry titan on a rampage.

Chance counted the chutes. The entire team was there. Now

he could focus and guide his descent to the agreed-upon location while following the path of the paracargo.

The gentle glide of the chute gave him too much time to think about the conversation he'd had with Maggie when he'd headed out that morning.

Her long blond hair had splayed across the pillow, mussed from sleep. Her body had pressed against his, warm and naked. She'd been more beautiful than he could ever remember.

He'd kissed her long and sweet. With his cock already hard and ready, he'd paused and stared into her sleepy eyes.

"Marry me," he blurted.

The minute he said the words, he knew he wanted this more than anything he'd ever wanted.

Instantly, her body stiffened, all sleep cleared from her eyes. "You know the answer." She shoved the sheets aside and sat up, scooting to the edge of the bed.

Chance grabbed her around the waist and held on, refusing to let her run. "I want you in my life."

"I told you from the start, I can't fall in love with or marry a jumper." She remained stiff, her body resisting his gentle tugging.

Chance sat up, his arms wrapping around her, his hands cupping her breasts. "Don't you like me? Just a little?" he said, trying to lighten the tension his sudden declaration left between them. He nibbled at the curve of her neck, tonguing the lobe of her ear before capturing it between his teeth.

"I work the base operations. I see what happens when a jumper doesn't return. I'm the one who has to notify loved ones that their husband or son will not be coming home—or will, but in a body bag. I won't be one of those people waiting on the sidelines for bad news. I can't."

"Who's to say I'll be one of those who doesn't make it? The

chances of dying on a jump are so slim, sweetheart. You know the statistics."

"I don't want to make that gamble." She struggled against him. "Let me go. I need to get back to my apartment."

"Okay, okay. I promise not to talk about marriage. Just don't leave yet. We can make love, then I'll cook breakfast. I'll make your favorite veggie omelet."

Her struggles slowed. "I should go."

"But you don't want to, not yet. Sex and an omelet...that's all I'm asking." *For now.* He'd have to work on her to get her to say yes to marriage. Prove to her that he was going to live long enough to grow old with her, raise a few kids, and hold his grandchildren. Yeah, Maggie Parker was worth the effort. She was the one for him.

She sighed and turned with a sad sort of smile. "You know the way to a girl's heart. Are you sure you don't want to feed me first?" Her tone deepened, the way it did when she was turned on. She got up on her hands and knees and straddled him. "I'm really hungry."

Food was the last thing on Chance's mind, with her pussy poised over his rock-hard dick. "Um, yeah, I'm hungry too."

She lowered herself so that the tip of his cock barely dipped into her warm, wet channel. Then she rose up, out of his reach. "Omelet-hungry or are you in the mood for something else? Shall I guess?" She dipped over him again, letting him in just a smidge deeper.

"You're killing me, woman."

"You're a big boy, you can handle it."

That she played and teased him when they made love was one of the things he found most endearing about Maggie. "I'm getting bigger all the time." He bucked, his hips rising, his cock reaching for her entrance.

Maggie slipped lower, down his body. His dick skimmed her belly. "Uh-uh. Not yet. I want a little appetizer before we start cooking." She inched down his chest, leaving a trail of kisses and tongue-flicks that had him so hot he thought he might ignite the sheets.

When Maggie's hands wrapped around his balls, Chance almost came right then. It took all his remaining self-control not to flip her over and ram himself deep into her cunt.

"My, my, aren't we hard this morning?" Her tongue touched the tip of his head, touching lightly against the slit at the end. "Umm, and I'm wet. Great condiment, don't you think?"

"I can't think at all when you do that," he said through gritted teeth.

"Then let me do the thinking...and tasting." She took him full into her mouth, the warmth and wetness so like her pussy.

Chance rose to fill her, thrusting deeper until the tip of his cock bumped the back of her throat.

All the while, she swirled her tongue around his hard length.

He could have come right then and there, but that wouldn't convince her to stay with him. Chance had to show her what she'd be getting if she chose him for life.

Once, twice, three times he thrust into her mouth, then he reached out, pulled her up over his body and rolled on top of her. "My turn for a little snack before breakfast." When she reached out for his ass, he grabbed her wrists and pinned them above her head. "Oh, no. I want it all, no distractions. Total focus is what I need."

"What? No multi-tasking? I thought all jumpers try to stay one step ahead of what they're doing."

"This particular kind of fire will take all my expertise and focus to control."

She wrapped her legs around his waist. "Think you can control this one?"

"Not a chance, but I'll give it my best." One hand gripping her wrists, the other unlacing her legs from around him, he ducked low, capturing a rosy-tipped breast between his teeth and nipping gently.

"Ouch." Instead of jerking away from his bite, Maggie arched her back, offering him more of the same.

He sucked her breast into his mouth, pulling hard.

Her heels dug into the mattress, her hips rising, eager to take him inside her. "Fuck me, jumper. Fuck me like this will be our last time."

"No way. It will be like it's the first of many more times. Every time we make love." He licked her nipple, releasing her wrists as he traveled down her body, his hand skimming across her flat belly to the thatch of soft, sandy-blond hair covering her pussy. His fingers threaded through the hairs, sliding between her folds. "I want you to want me as much as I do you."

"In case you haven't noticed..." She cupped his hand and pushed it lower to her heated, moist entrance. "I already do want you."

"Not enough." Not enough to say she'd stay with him for always. "I want you to scream for more."

"I don't scream," she replied, her tone haughty.

"You will." He kissed her belly, his finger sliding into her pussy. "You will." He used the wet finger to slide over her clit, deftly flicking the nubbin with just enough pressure to tease.

"No..." She drew in a sharp breath.

He flicked again.

"I won't..." her breath hitched, "screeeeeaaammmm!"

"Close enough." He grinned up at her. "I'd call that a scream." Before she could force enough air into her lungs to argue, he slid his tongue in between her folds where his finger had just been.

Her heels pushed against the mattress, and she rose to meet him, encouraging him to continue.

He did, sucking her clit into his mouth, twirling on the swollen tip with his tongue.

"Now, now!" she screamed, her hips pushing higher, her body shuddering with her release.

One final lick at her sweet spot, and he swiftly climbed up her body and slammed home, his cock sliding in her well-slickened channel. He buried himself all the way to the hilt, drawing out halfway, then thrusting in again and again, riding her with fast, steady strokes that made her crazed enough to explode with another wave of orgasm.

Maggie wrapped her legs around his middle, locking her ankles, her heels digging into his ass.

As the first wave of release hit, he almost hesitated. If he shot his wad into her, he could impregnate her. Then she'd have to marry him. For a flash of a second, he imagined her big with his child. As quickly as the image rose, it was consumed by another. Maggie big with child, waiting for him to return from a fire. Sick with worry.

Chance pulled free at the last moment, his sperm squirting out across her belly. No, he wouldn't trick her into marriage, and he didn't want her to carry his child, living in the shadow of fear that he might not return to see his baby grow up.

Maggie was right. She shouldn't be fool enough to fall in love with a jumper and most definitely, she shouldn't marry one. In most likelihood, it would only end in heartbreak for her.

After a long, sexy shower where they made love all over again, Chance fixed Maggie's omelet. When she'd kissed him goodbye and told him she didn't want to see him anymore, he didn't argue. He took it on the chin, knowing she was doing the right thing.

Then why the hell did it hurt so much?

What other choice did he have?

Not an hour later, Chance, Maggie, and twenty other smoke jumpers and ground support personnel had been called into action.

Now, as he fell toward the earth, he could think of the only choice he had if he wanted to keep Maggie in his life. He could quit or request a desk job with the forest service and spend his days pushing pencils, trapped in a safe, air-conditioned office throughout his youth, hating his life and resenting having given up jumping to become a family man. Then again, he couldn't imagine hating his life too much if Maggie was in it.

Chance adjusted his chute as the ground rushed up to meet him, landing gently, knees bent to take the impact. He pushed thoughts of Maggie to the back of his mind, concentrating all his energy and strength on saving the lives and property of hundreds of people and possibly thousands of animals.

As the day progressed into night, he didn't need a flashlight to see what he was doing. While he and the other jumpers battled to establish a firebreak on the opposite side of a stream, the fire raged on, burning a path directly for them. The clouds they'd seen on the horizon hadn't materialized to push their way across the horizon to quench the fire, as the firefighters had hoped and prayed. It was up to them to do their best to stop the blaze from spreading farther.

Maggie manned the operations center, anticipating resupply and providing first aid to injured firefighters as they were brought in by truck or helicopter. The night lengthened into morning with no sign of the fire letting up. It continued to burn unchecked, closing in on the jumpers' location faster than anyone had anticipated.

She'd kept one ear cocked for the radio operator, praying for news from the team that had set up across a stream. The strike team leader had checked in when they'd all landed safely and located the paracargo box full of supplies. That had been the last contact they'd had from Chance's team. No one had heard from them for more than eighteen hours. The shift supervisor had begun to worry. Dozens of planes had dropped fire-retardant material on the flames, but the wind hadn't let up. The dead and diseased trees acted as kindling, making it easier for the flames to leap from branch to branch, leaving a charred and blackened earth in their wake.

Maggie tended the wounded, fixed coffee, and handed out sandwiches as shifts changed—and still no word from Chance.

The previous morning she'd had every intention of ending their relationship; she couldn't risk falling in love with a jumper.

This morning, after she'd spent more than twenty-four hours on her feet worrying, she'd come to the realization that it was too late. She'd been in love with Chance from the day he'd swaggered through the door of the station, his jumpsuit black with soot, his face gray with ash. His blue eyes had been slightly red-rimmed, but shining as bright as his teeth when he gave her a cocky grin and asked her out on a date.

She'd had it on the tip of her tongue to tell him where to go. But when his buddy mocked him for asking a girl out when he looked as bad as he did, she'd taken him up on the offer, soot and all.

That had been three months ago. The past twenty-four hours might as well have been three months, as slow as the time had stretched.

Then a *ping, ping, ping* echoing off the station's metal roof jerked her back to the present. She ran outside and stared up at the sky full of dark gray clouds as they released a torrent of rain.

She laughed and raised her arms to the soggy heavens and thanked the Lord for His help in quenching the fire.

The rain took its time sweeping across the Idaho mountains and valleys. As it did, teams reported in, one by one, that the fire was out. Jumpers were recalled; trucks picked some up. Helicopters swooped in and collected the more remote teams and their equipment.

Maggie treated, assessed, and arranged for transport for the more seriously injured, all the while praying she'd see Chance step through the door, all full of attitude and wearing his beautiful cocky grin.

By the end of the day, Maggie had been up for more than thirty-six hours. Her back ached, her feet burned, and still no sign of Chance. When his strike team leader stuck his head in the door to report their return, Maggie almost cried. She rushed out into the parking lot, her gaze searching for Chance.

"You're not going to find Muldoon here." Randy, one of Chance's teammates found her standing in the rain, crying.

Lead sank to the pit of her belly before she remembered that the strike team leader had reported they were all there and accounted for. Maggie grabbed Randy's collar and pulled him close. "Then where the hell is he?"

"Hey, hey. He's okay." Randy smiled and pointed toward the road. "He said something about a cool stream just down the road. You know the one. Some of the guys like to swim there."

Her shift had ended hours before. Maggie ducked into the building, told her boss she'd be leaving, and ran down the road to the stream, less than half a mile away.

When she got there, she still didn't see Chance anywhere. "Muldoon!" she yelled.

No one responded. Had he gotten down here and had a latent

reaction to smoke inhalation? Would she find him gagging for air, or worse, already unconscious?

She followed the stream, working her way up a hillside, slowly at first. Then she was running, afraid she'd be too late. Maggie tripped and fell through a break in the brush, tears falling, her hands stinging where she'd landed on sticks and rocks. When she looked up, she spotted a soaking wet jumpsuit spread out across a rock, boots set neatly in front of the boulder.

She scrambled to her feet and peered over the top of the big stone to discover a lovely little waterfall and a smooth, clear pool of water surrounded by dense green forest. Beneath the tumble of water stood Chance, his naked body gleaming and wet.

Without thinking, Maggie, ran along the edge of the pool, relief bringing more tears to her eyes. He was alive. "Chance!"

He didn't turn. He probably couldn't hear her with the water rushing around his hears.

Maggie plowed into the pool, water up to her knees. When she reached him, she flung her arms around him, burying her face against his back, the pounding of the waterfall washing away her tears. "Thank God. Oh, thank God," she said, coughing when she snorted a lungful of water.

Chance turned and pushed her out of the full force of the waterfall. "Maggie. Oh, sweet Maggie. Of course I'm all right." He held her close, his arms tight around her middle, his cock pressing into her belly, already halfway hard.

"I was so worried. Dear God, I thought I'd die." Maggie glanced up into his face. "I was afraid I wouldn't get to tell you."

"Tell me what?"

"It's too late," she babbled, too happy to be coherent.

"Too late?" Chance held her at arm's length. "Too late for what?"

"It's too late. I promised I wouldn't fall in love with a jumper." She sobbed, trying to get close enough to press herself against his chest, but he wouldn't let her, holding her back.

"You're right, Maggie. You deserve a man you don't have to worry about. A man who'll be around for you, help you raise children, grow old with you."

Maggie sighed. "Got one in mind?" She looked up at him, her hair hanging wet and limp in her face. God, she must be a mess. "I was wrong this morning."

"Yesterday morning?"

She laughed, the sound ending on a sob. "I want to keep on seeing you. I want to be a part of your life."

"And I want you to be, and I want to be that guy who's there for you."

"You do?" She smiled. "You didn't change your mind?"

"Far from it." He smoothed a wet strand out of her eyes. "I'm going to ask for a transfer to a desk job."

"What?" Maggie shook her head. "You can't do that. Being a jumper is what you do, who you are. If you quit jumping before your time, you'll hate it." She hugged him around the middle. "Being a jumper is what made me fall in love with you from the first time I saw you. You stop fires, you save lives. What woman wouldn't want a hero like that?"

Chance's brows furrowed. "But you said you'd never fall in love with a jumper."

She cupped his cheek in her palm and stared into his eyes. "We don't always get to choose who we fall in love with, and I wouldn't change one thing about you."

"What about the worry? What if I don't come back from a jump?"

"Shhh. Don't say that." She pressed a finger to his lips. "I promise not to borrow trouble. I want to cherish the time I have with you, whether it's a minute, an hour, or the rest of our lives. I love you, Chance Muldoon."

"It's a good thing. Otherwise, I'd have to step back under the waterfall to keep from doing this." He scooped her legs from under her and wrapped them around his middle.

Maggie laughed and clung to him. "Aren't you forgetting something?"

He tapped her trouser-clad bottom with his cock and grinned. "Right as usual." With less grace than eagerness, he dropped her to her feet and dragged her trousers and panties off her legs, dunking her in the process. He slung the garments toward the rocks, lining the edges of the pool. Then he pulled her shirt over her head, unclipped her bra, and sent them flying with the rest, leaving her standing there in front of him just as naked as he was. "Are you sure this is what you want?"

She laced her hands behind his neck and dragged his face close to hers. "Absolutely."

As his lips descended to claim hers, he scooped her up by the backs of her legs.

She wrapped them around his middle and lowered herself onto his thick, wet cock. Maggie couldn't deny her love for this man any more than she could stop breathing. So what if he jumped into harm's way? He was her jumper.

Chance backed her against a rock ledge, balancing her on its stony surface as he thrust in and out. When his body grew rigid, she clung to his shoulders, her ankles locking behind him, hanging on the edge of an earth-shaking orgasm. She didn't want him to pull free. She knew that, at last, and embraced the potential consequences of what might happen.

He froze, his face set in tense, barely controlled lines. "Are you sure?"

She nodded.

"I love you, Maggie Parker." Then he thrust once more and came in sync with her own release, his cock throbbing inside her.

Breathless and completely satisfied, she laughed when he lifted her from the rock and stepped beneath the waterfall to do it all again.

This was her life with her very own smoke jumper, and she wouldn't have it any other way.

STOKE

Tahira Iqbal

I don't know how or why but suddenly smoke is billowing out of the hood of my car. I've blown a gasket before, but the color of the smoke...it's different, it's darker...more dangerous. Flames start to flicker from under the hood, pushing up and out through the front of the grill. Oh, dear God. It's definitely not the gasket. I pull over.

Moving quickly, I grab my handbag before popping open the door and stumbling out onto the quiet country lane. I should have been at work by now—my shift starts at midnight. Without the moon, the only light is from the headlights. I stand in their arcs, lifting out my cell to call emergency services, fingers barely able to dial. The calm, controlled voice on the other end urges me to get as far away from the vehicle as possible and assures me help is on the way.

I'm about ten meters away when the flames grow, blooming into a bulbous cloud, followed quickly by an ear-splitting boom. Propelled off my feet, I'm flung backward as the car explodes.

Utterly dazed, I try to sit up, having landed awkwardly on the grass by the side of the road. I look at the old Chevy as I back myself against a tree trunk, pressing my spine against it and hugging my knees. The only thought running through my mind is that I was in that car no more than a couple of minutes ago. And everything inside me goes still with shock.

Sirens. Lots of them. Doors opening, closing. Voices…loud, clear. Calm. I haven't opened my eyes. I can't… The heat from the car stings my skin even from this distance.

"Ma'am."

A reassuringly masculine voice reaches inside, creating an echo that offers a comfort I've never known before.

"Ma'am, can you hear me?" The presence kneels beside me, placing a hand on my shoulder. "It's okay… You can open your eyes."

Warm hands slide into mine; the touch makes me do what he asks.

"Welcome back."

My gaze is on the smoldering wreck. A group of his colleagues surround it, dousing it with powerful jets of foam, making it look like it's covered in liquid snow.

"It's totaled," I whisper, looking up at the voice, the man clearly visible in the flashing lights. The reflective stripes on his yellow uniform catch them. I close my eyes against the light show.

"Hey, you there?" His hand touches my shoulder.

"I was in the car…" I mumble, looking up at him, his wonderfully dark eyes twitching with concern.

"I know. But you made it out okay, just hold onto that."

A paramedic comes over.

"All right now, Jim will take good care of you."

This new firefighter's clean-shaven and wears a smile that would melt a nun's heart.

I accept the foil blanket, smiling at Jim as we've worked together for years at the ER. His wise blue eyes look troubled.

"Thank you," I whisper to the stranger. He pulls his thick gloves back on and jogs to my car to assist. I'm led away to the ambulance by Jim, my legs trembling.

"Jesus Christ!" My friend and colleague, Drew, comes rushing around from the reception desk. "Curtain four is open!"

Jim walks me through the ER quickly. Drew's hand is at my elbow for additional support.

I nod meekly at the desk staff who are all on their feet staring at me. Lucy, the receptionist, puts her hand to her mouth, her eyes pooling with tears.

I swallow back a lump of emotion. "I'm fine," I whisper.

Once I'm levered onto the bed, Drew works quickly, checking my pupils, blood pressure, and everything in between.

Anna, who I like to call my work mom, hovers beside me, locating and passing equipment to Drew and the other nurses, who work professionally beside me in an alert state of silence.

The man is unflappable in the face of crisis, but even he's ashen. "God, you could have been killed. I've been telling you that car was a death trap!"

"I know," I say quietly, thumbing away the tears. "God! I should be able to cope with this. I'm a nurse, I'm used to these situations!"

"Honey," Anna says softly, "it's happened to you, so the rulebook goes out the window."

I close my eyes. Inhale. Exhale. Seeing nothing but the firefighter standing near the shell of my smoking car, watching as Jim helps me into the back of the ambulance.

Later I protest against the CT scan, but it's lost against the chorus of concern—even though I'm sure I didn't bump my head when I landed on the grass. Soon I'm being wheeled out of the cubicle. My body is ringing, but I'm mercifully uninjured, although I'm sure bruises will form. The scan comes back clear of any hidden injury; the nurse in me knew that would be the case.

"There's a guy in reception asking for you." Lucy pops her head through the curtain later in the night. "He's kinda hot."

"Kinda hot and asking for me?" I mumble, hugging the covers, "he's clearly lost." The drugs have kicked in, warming me within. "Send the handsome stranger in."

Lucy leaves, the curtains rustling as she goes.

I must have dozed off because the next thing I *feel* is his presence. It's magnetic…familiar.

My eyes fly open.

"You look better," he says, clearly off duty, wearing jeans that cover muscular legs, a black shirt open at the throat, with a matching jacket… But he's carrying a handbag.

My gaze darts to his.

"This is yours, not mine. Promise!" He laughs.

I almost don't recognize the tan leather tote. It's muddied beyond recognition.

He sets it on the chair. "Your phone kept ringing, so I thought I'd bring it to you."

"That's…" I try to sit up, but the bed has been lowered halfway to the prone position to help me get some rest.

"Let me."

He moves easily, reaching back and adjusting the bed so that I can be upright. I get a whiff of his cologne as he steps away. It's dauntingly male.

"You were lucky."

I nod shakily, my spine pricking with the memories.

"Well, I'll leave you to get some rest."

"Oh, okay... Um, thank you, again." I gesture to the bag.

"No problem, ma'am."

"Aida, my name is Aida."

He extends his hand. "Nick."

We connect. Our eyes meet again.

His smile grows. "Aida," he whispers quietly, his eyes brightening.

The curtain rattles, startling me. It's Drew.

"I'll leave you to it. Feel better." Nick leaves through the gap, passing Drew, who is wearing a grin as wide as the sun.

In the end, I'm kept overnight.

"Ready?"

Drew is giving me a ride home, and as I walk into the morning sunshine, I can't help but squint. I reach into my bag for my shades. I'm wearing pale blue scrubs, and Lucy let me borrow her denim jacket. Anna took my clothes to her house to launder.

I fish around inside my bag, groaning as I discover that it's damp. And oh...my shades are broken; one of the arms has snapped off.

"I don't think I can give you a ride home," Drew murmurs.

"What? Why?"

I look at Drew, but he's smirking like a kid. He nods toward the parking lot.

I follow his line of sight. Oh my... It's Nick, casually leaning against the bonnet of his SUV, and once he sees us, he heads in my direction.

"Aida, I was wondering if I could take you out for breakfast? If you're feeling up to it?"

Drew is practically jumping up and down beside me. "Sure you can. She's fine, aren't you?"

"Andrew!" I bat his arm.

Nick just smiles, clearly enjoying my blush.

"I'll leave her in your capable hands," Drew says, making me blush again. He walks away, giving me the "call me" sign behind Nick's back.

But in the act of looking up, I collide with the sunshine. I squeeze my eyes shut.

"You don't feel so good?"

"No... I'm fine." I hold up my sunglasses in explanation. "I didn't get much sleep."

Nick plucks his own pair from the vee of his white T-shirt and puts the aviator-style shades on the bridge of my nose. "There. That better?"

"Better," I whisper hoarsely, affected by the gesture.

We drive through town, heading north.

"Could we go someplace else?" I ask, as he pulls into a vacant parking spot and I realize where we are.

"Sure."

"What, no questions?"

"You must have a valid reason for asking."

I smile, studying him freely from behind the shades. The car is big, but he still fills it out nicely. One big hand rests on the gear, the other on the wheel. He has neatly trimmed black hair. It's almost the same shade as mine.

"Aida?"

I stop staring and regroup. "It's just half of the night shift will be in there eating breakfast, including Drew. I could do without the... You know."

His laugh heats me up in places that have been cold for a seriously long time.

"Okay. I know a place."

Ten minutes later, we arrive at a block of apartments.

"I live on the top floor, and there's no elevator," he says, looking worried.

I peer up at the well maintained block. "I'll be fine." I slide the sunglasses off as we head through the communal door.

Nick jogs effortlessly up the stairs, while I have to grip the banister by the second floor.

"I could carry you over my shoulder."

"Nothing's on fire." I look up at him as he waits on the landing.

"Are you sure?" He gives me a scorching smile.

I restart my climb with vigor, my inner thighs tingling.

His apartment is small and surprisingly neat.

"Did you just transfer to the firehouse?"

"Yeah." Nick shrugs out of his jacket. "How did you figure that out?"

"I know most of the guys. They're usually flowing through the ER on shouts. Is Murphy giving you hell?"

He smirks. "He did for about the first hour."

"You went up against Murphy? I'm impressed," I say as he disappears into the kitchen while I stride to the living-room window.

"Here you go."

I accept the bottle of water, nodding my thanks.

"Did the doc give you painkillers?"

"Yes."

"Do you need to take them?"

"I'm okay."

"Don't be a hero."

"I'm fine." I pop the cap and take a sip.

Nick watches me, his hazel gaze steeping with color.

"Do you follow up with all the women you rescue?" I try to calm the nerves within. No one has ever looked at me *that* way before.

His sexy smile brightens the room. "No, just you." Nick takes the opportunity to trace his finger down my cheek.

The sun suddenly dips behind cloud cover. It takes my mood with it. Oh my God...my car caught fire... I was sitting in the car...watching the flames... What if I hadn't gotten out?

"Hey...hey..." Nick rubs the side of my arm. "You okay?"

"Um...do you think you could take me home?" I try to hide the quiver in my voice.

"Sure." Concern is written in his lowering brow. "It's hitting you, isn't it?"

I nod, and that's when the tears start to trail down my cheeks.

Nick leans in and he does the sexiest thing a man has ever done to me—he kisses away the tears.

We drive in quiet, just the radio playing the latest hits softly in the background. I fight the need to sleep, which has been made even more challenging because Nick's given me his jacket to ward off the chill I'm feeling. It's far too big, but I've got it wrapped around my shoulders over Lucy's. I can't help but savor the scent of his cologne. I want to close my eyes, drift toward rest, but all too soon we're on my street.

I turn to Nick. "I'm sorry."

He shakes his head. "For what?"

"For flaking out."

"Aida, you were in a pretty serious accident. It's a natural reaction."

Unsure of what to say, I slide the jacket off my shoulders.

"Keep it for now," he says. "It gives me a reason to come by and see you again." Nick leans in, gently pressing his lips against mine. "I've wanted to do that since the moment I laid eyes on you. I've never felt that drawn to a stranger before, and when you opened your eyes..."

He trails off, so I just press my forehead against his before he walks me to my door.

Nick moves comfortably around my open kitchen, investigating the cupboards until he locates a glass, then filling it with water so that I can take the painkillers.

"I don't feel good about leaving you alone."

"I have Cooper." I'm sitting at the dining table.

That seems to knock the wind out of his sails. Those wonderful eyes dim.

Mine widen. "No, Cooper's my dog!"

Color seeps back into his face.

Oh... I like that...

"He's probably sleeping. He's a night owl."

"Like you?" Nick hunkers down before me. "So, technically, you should be sleeping right about now?" His voice has dropped to a sexy, suggestive whisper.

My lips part and a powerful warmth inside has me leaning toward him.

"You need a few hours in bed," he says firmly.

I'm on my feet before I know it.

He catches the twinkle in my eye. "To sleep."

"What?" Did I whine?

His smile is soft. "You heard me... You need your rest."

I would argue with him, but he's right. My body clock is wired for night shifts this week. Plus I've got a tension headache, and my body is starting to stiffen up. Sex with the sexy stranger might just have to wait.

We go to my room where he lifts the covers off the bed and helps me under them. I mumble that I'll be fine, and he can go.

"You've got a head injury, and last time I checked, dogs can't use phones. I'll stick around to check on you every couple of hours."

A kiss meets my temple, and I fall into a comforting sleep.

I wake at two PM to energetic shouting coming from my small garden. I rise, going to the window.

There's Cooper chasing a ball. Nick claps his hands, bringing the black Lab back to his feet. He rubs Cooper's head before extracting the ball from his jaw and tossing it toward the back fence.

"You've made a friend." I step out from the kitchen onto the small decked area.

"You're up. Feel better?"

"Yes, thank you," I say. "Hey, Cooper." He totally ignores me and heads for Nick. "Oh, that's nice!"

Nick tosses the ball again, laughing. "I made something to eat. Hope you don't mind."

"You found something edible in my fridge?"

"No, but your pantry was pretty decent." Cooper barks, telling Nick he's back with the ball. "Hey buddy, I'm going to take care of Aida now, okay?"

The dog gets another pat, follows us in, and heads for the couch, where he jumps up, resting his head on his paws, to watch us in the kitchen.

Nick reaches for plates and dishes up the pasta he's made. Ten minutes and two delicious servings later, I'm full.

Assured that I'm better, Nick leaves me with the pot of pasta. He softly kisses me goodbye at the door, and I watch, smiling, as his SUV disappears down the street.

I retreat to bed, taking my cell with me. I have thirteen texts and a voicemail. I don't even need to check it to know that it's Drew asking for details. I also get a call from my sister. Somehow she has sensed that something happened. She's two thousand miles away and I don't want to worry her, but she gets the story out of me. Assuring her that I'm fine just does not work; she's going to be on the next flight.

I respond to everyone with a group message, thanking them for their get-well-soon wishes, and call Drew, but end up having to leave a voicemail. I tuck myself into bed, Cooper at my feet. My dog is clearly wondering where his new friend is, because the ball is sitting beside him.

It's eleven PM by the time Marianne arrives.

She hugs me hard at the door and wheels in her small case, her bottle blonde hair rolled in a bun. She's still in her work suit. "Thank God you're okay!"

Her big, brown eyes fill with even more tears as I tell her what happened and how Nick has taken care of me.

We head back to my room to sleep after she heats some of the pasta for herself and we catch up. I wake at four AM, totally alert and *oh!* so stiff and sore!

I find that I've got a nasty bruise the size of a dinner plate on my left hip and other small marks dotted around my body.

I stretch carefully, groaning as I get out of bed and wander through the house to retrieve my cell from the kitchen counter. There's a text from Nick.

Lunch at Brand's, say noon? I'm guessing you're not going into work? I can pick you up? Or I can come to you and find something in that pantry?

Smiling, I text him back. My boss urged me to take some time off to get better. I'd protested at first, but perhaps it's a good thing now that Marianne is here—and Nick has arrived into my life, lifting the unease that I can't help but feel.

Lunch at Brand's sounds great. My sister is here; she can drop me off. See you soon.

"Why are you grinning like an idiot?"

I turn around to find Marianne in her PJs, rubbing her eyes.

"I have a date." I hold up my cell.

She smiles, "With pasta man? Thank God. I thought you were going to be single forever."

I get a sleepy hug before she heads back to bed.

Marianne drops me off at Brand's later that day. "You got everything?"

I turn to face her. "You sound like Mom."

"Honey, I'm not talking about your lunch money. Protection, you got it?"

"Marianne!"

She wrinkles her nose. "We're both grownups, and the way that tall piece of holy-God hotness is looking at you, you're not going to be upright for very long."

Nick walks to my door, opens it, and extends his hand.

I really hope he doesn't notice my blush. "I'll see you later," I say to my sis without looking her way. I take his hand and ease out as Nick greets Marianne politely.

We head into Brand's. I search for an empty table.

"I thought we could get takeout and go eat outside."

We stroll slowly up the road, towards Amber Park, taking a bench facing the water. It's a lovely sunny day. Nick's given me his shades again.

I eat the sandwich and sip the fresh lemonade, "Was today your day off?"

"Yeah, in fact, I've got the weekend off."

I smile with anticipation, sipping through the straw.

"I've got plans, though."

"Oh," I murmur, disappointment impossible to keep from my expression.

"With you," he says.

I fight my smile.

"I know your sister is in town, but how about I look after

you for the next couple of days?"

I don't get to answer his question as fat lashes of rain start to fall. We head back to the car, my body protesting as I try for a run, but end up walking.

"If I asked you to pack a bag and come with me..." He's driven me back home, thunder rumbling overhead. The shades are back in his vee. "Would you do it?"

"Wow. You're a really organized serial killer." I'm damp from the rain...and from his words, as they snake through my pelvis and hit home.

He laughs before fishing out his cell, flicking through his email. "To prove I'm not crazy."

I take the cell. There's an email confirmation for a hotel booking.

"If it's too fast, then you..."

"No, it's just..." I exhale softly, "it's..."

"I want to make love to you...but if I do it in my apartment, everyone's going to know what I'm doing and this town... It's small." His voice is soft, but charged. And oh God...now his lips are against my neck. "Say yes..."

An hour later, I've got a bag packed and I'm waving to a bemused Marianne, who's standing at the front door with a pissed-off Cooper. I recall the conversation she had with Nick.

"I want a copy of that email, your cell number, full name, address, employer..."

"Yes ma'am," Nick says seriously, plucking out his cell. "I plan on taking very good care of your sister."

"You bloody well better." She grabs her buzzing cell and reads the details. "Nicholas Henry Forbes."

"Never mess with a kick-ass lawyer," I whisper to him as we walk down the path, but he just kisses the tip of my nose, whispering back that he doesn't mind.

The drive takes just under an hour. Nick wraps his free hand around my waist, escorting me inside the quaint bed-and-breakfast. We check in, but head back out into the parking lot with our key.

"We're not going to the room?"

"We're staying in one of those." He points in the direction of the beach.

I see numerous two-story detached cottages dotted along it. The surf crashes against the sand making me feel incredibly relaxed and well.

"Like I said...we're going to make some noise." He kisses me. His lips are hard and full of need, and leave me shuddering inside.

He dumps our bags inside the door before reaching for me, his finger under my chin, lifting it until we meet each other's gazes. I hadn't realized how tall he is. I'm five-nine, and I've got to really look up at him.

Nick's lips find mine, pressing softly. I open my mouth to welcome him in, awed by the sense of security I'm feeling emanating from him.

Everything lights up within as he reaches under my shirt to flatten his palms against bare skin.

I moan into his mouth as his fingers accidently graze the bruise. I break away to recapture my breath.

He kisses me delicately, once more on the lips, before we head up the stairs.

The bedroom is gorgeous and faces the ocean. The bed is dressed in whites, with accents of stone grey and sand to bring the outside in.

Nick removes his shirt first, making me catch my breath. His job depends on his strength. There's nothing sexier than a man who cares not only for the people he saves, but for himself—his body is ripped like a pro footballer's.

I reach for his belt buckle, unclasping it and drawing it out from the loops.

Nick reaches for my jacket, pushing it off my shoulders before sending my T-shirt to the pile of clothes we're making at our feet.

I pop all the buttons of his fly, putting my fingers into the waistband, pushing until the denims hit the floor. He steps out of them and his sneakers, looking like a model in his Calvin Kleins.

I get out of my denims and flats, standing before him in my black bra and panties, aware of the decent-sized bulge in his white briefs.

His eyes travel down my body. "You're hurt. Why didn't you say?" Nick drops to his knees…and suddenly his lips are pressing softly on my bruised hip bone.

I sway where I stand, partially exploding inside from the sensations. I plant my hands on his shoulders.

Then…oh God…he's taking off my panties, and his tongue is soon pressing against my wet seam.

I grip his shoulders harder, desperate to remain standing as nothing but euphoric gasps escape from my mouth.

Soon, he's guiding me to the bed. I watch as he rolls on a condom, and leaning over me, mindful of my hip, he drives himself slowly deep inside of me.

He's like no other lover I've ever had, and he's confident about the welcome he's going to receive from my body, because I'm parting my legs, ignoring the complaints of my flesh.

He pushes in deeply, settling there until I've accepted his significant presence with a soft, mewing moan.

Kisses rain down on my lips, and I taste myself. I give up on gripping the sheets and wrap my hands around his waist to pull him closer, unable to stop from panting his name.

"I want to hear you." He pulls out and thrusts back in, pushing me toward an orgasm that has me arching my back and moaning as the bruises tingle.

I press my breasts into his chest as he slides his hands into my hair, my panting loud, loud...then louder.

Carefully he holds my head in place, kissing me as my body blasts into a thrilling tempest of an orgasm. I can't help but yell his name.

"It was loud...but not loud enough." He kisses me hard, smiling and out of breath. "Round two... You feel okay?"

I nod as he maneuvers me carefully onto all fours, and I'm screaming his name in seconds.

When I wake, he's not beside me, and the bed is cold. Wrapping myself in a sheet, I follow my nose and head slowly downstairs. "You're cooking?"

He's wearing just his sweatpants as he stands at the stove. "Did you bring the food?"

"I did."

I peck him on the side of his shoulder in thanks before taking a bar stool. I lift a small bottle of mineral water from the welcome basket.

"I got a text from your sister."

I spit out my water.

"She spoke to my boss and got a reference confirming I was an upstanding citizen." His smile is wry. His eyes dance.

I wipe my mouth with the back of my hand, mumbling an apology, but Nick just kisses my hair as he comes around with plates of steak and salad.

After we've eaten, we dress and take a stroll on the beach as dusk hits the horizon.

Nick's got his arm draped around my shoulder and I've got

his jacket on again to ward off the chill.

"I can't believe this place is only an hour from town." I sigh with contentment, the stiffness from the accident mingling with the aftereffects of energetic sex.

"Easy to get to for other weekends."

"There are going to be other weekends?"

"I hope so." Nick kisses the top of my head. "I really hope so."

SOMETHING'S BURNING

Cynthia D'Alba

B eef fat oozed off the grill onto charcoal briquettes, exciting the flames to lick hungrily at the undersides of expensive sirloin patties.

"Damn it, damn it, *damn it*," Bree Hardy yelled as she grabbed for the garden hose coiled on the concrete patio. A pitiful stream of water dribbled out when she squeezed the nozzle handle. Whipping her gaze toward the water spigot, she watched as most of the water gushed from a large hole in the hose.

"Damn it!" She sprinted to her kitchen for a pitcher of water then raced back to the grill. Standing a couple of feet from the flames, she tossed the water toward the fire. Too late to salvage her dinner. The chopped sirloin burgers were now disks of crusty black char.

Sighing, she shoved sweaty hair off her forehead as she waited for her galloping heart to slow to a trot. Why couldn't she get the hang of grilling? Men did it every day. She could do anything a man could do.

The charred meat patties clanked as she shoveled them onto a glass plate. She left the plate on a redwood picnic table while she slowly slid the grill lid over the base holding the smoldering coals. Her heart and lungs worked overtime as she stepped backward away from the fire-breathing dragon. When would she get over this childish fear of fire?

Did she need another pitcher of water from the kitchen to thoroughly drown the remaining embers? The fire was contained in a metal base designed to hold it. She was being ridiculous.

But the last thing she wanted was a house fire. Carefully, she rolled the charcoal grill off the patio as far from her back door as physically possible. At this safety move, she sighed with relief.

The hamburger platter jiggled in her shaking hands when she picked it up and headed for her townhouse. Her three-year-old border collie Gracie—the recipient of all her failed grilling exercises—nipped happily at Bree's toes as though to say "Hurry up and feed it to me."

The French door rattled when she slammed it in disgust—at her foolish fear, her inept cooking, and, most importantly, her failure to go grocery shopping. Setting the charred burgers on the counter, Bree glanced toward the dog quivering in anticipation. "Well, at least one of us gets hamburger tonight." She tossed Gracie a chunk of charred meat before mixing more with a healthy dose of kibble.

She leaned against the counter and allowed herself a full minute of self-pity. Her lack of cooking skills was ridiculous. Damn it, she was a doctor. She knew every muscle and blood vessel in the human body, understood disease symptoms and cures. She was smart—and she'd be damned if she'd let something like using a simple grill get the best of her.

But that would have to wait for another night. The hour was

getting late. Her day had started at seven with hospital rounds and ended at seven with another set. She was tired and hungry and grumpy.

Bree grabbed the telephone receiver and pushed the speed dial.

"Wong's," the voice on the phone answered.

"Hi. It's Bree Hardy. I need to place an order for delivery."

"You want the usual, Dr. Hardy?"

"Sure. But this time, extra sweet and sour sauce."

"Be there in thirty."

Her wait began for her Chinese dinner of sweet and sour chicken with an egg roll side order.

She wrapped the charred burgers in foil and put them in the refrigerator for Gracie's dinners later in the week. The acidic smell of smoke nauseated her. Each breath brought a new whiff. It'd be at least twenty more minutes until her dinner arrived. Plenty of time to shower and get the smell out of her hair.

Holding a glass of Pinot Grigio, she headed up the stairs. Gracie bounded up right behind her and sat on the shower mat. Bree turned on the water to get the hot going while she stripped out of her shorts and T-shirt. While she scrubbed, Bree lamented the sad state of her love life. No dates with anyone interesting. She feared she would jump the first good-looking man who asked her out.

As she pictured the male hunk one yard over, she shivered. If she could get his attention...oh, yummy. So far he'd nodded a couple of times as they passed, but that was the extent of his display of interest. Not promising.

With a twist of the ring, she changed the shower massager from needle spray to alternating pounding jets. Hot water hammered down on her shoulders. Placing both hands on the shower wall, she stretched and twisted her back and neck in a vain attempt to convince her knotted muscles to give up their tension. Her head sagged. Long, sopping hair slapped the wet flesh of her breasts and belly.

The muscle tension held on. Maybe if the water were hotter. Or maybe the strike of the pulsing water against her flesh needed to be stronger or closer or something. She twisted the dial until the water was hot enough to dilate the blood vessels in any area it touched.

Lifting the handheld shower head from its holder, she brought the power of the jets closer to her neck. The shower head moved side to side, and the stiffness in her shoulders gave way to the soothing water massage.

A sharp stream of water shot over her shoulder, striking her nipple, bringing it to full erection. A streak of painful pleasure shot down to her clit. She moaned in delight and brought the showerhead directly to her breasts, forcing the hard jets of water to strike each nipple sharply. Her body tensed in response, sexual tension racing from her head to her toes.

She lowered the pulsing stream to her abdomen, the hot water not calming but inciting her muscles to quiver in response. She spread her legs wider. Hot streams of water shot through the curly hair at the apex of her thighs and dripped off the swollen lips of her vulva. When a second low moan escaped her throat, she gritted her teeth.

Moving the showerhead between her legs, she let the pulsing streams pound at the throb inside her. Her thigh muscles quivered and shook as she moved the pulsating jets back and forth, from her clitoris between the lips covering her vagina to her anus and back to the rigid nub of her sex.

A glance through the glass shower door caught her reflection in the mirror. Wet hair tangled and wild-looking. Standing on her toes, legs spread. One hand supporting the showerhead striking water between her legs, the other plucking a taut nipple. She moaned, catching her lower lip with her teeth.

Inside, the pressure mounted, demanding release. Her breaths came in shallow, rapid pants. A hard jet of water hit her clit. Her body jerked in response. Finally, the building internal heaviness overflowed. A sense of dizziness swept through her. Shocking white lights flashed behind her closed eyelids.

Her body too overwhelmed to take more stimulation, she jerked the showerhead away. Quake after quake rattled through her system until she was limp with sexual release. She replaced the showerhead into its holder and let the water wash over her sated body until she could stand without holding onto the shower wall. She stepped from the shower.

Gracie licked the water droplets from Bree's legs.

"Stop it," she demanded as Gracie's tongue tickled behind her knee. Now, if the guy next door wanted to do that...

Bree sighed and reached for the wineglass on the sink. Just as she lifted it to her mouth, she heard a loud crash and shout.

"Aw, shit. Fire!"

Intrigued, she stepped to the bathroom window and shoved it open. She looked in the direction of the roar—her backyard— and spotted a six-foot section of her privacy fence collapsing in roiling flames as the hunky neighbor in the adjacent yard ran for his garden hose.

With a gasp, she grabbed a short pink silk robe off the bathroom door and hustled down the stairs. Grabbing the water pitcher off the counter, she filled it with water from the kitchen faucet and ran onto the patio. Intense heat slammed into her face, sucking the breath from her lungs as she neared the fence inferno. She tossed the pitcherful of water onto the fire, but the effort was like putting a Band-Aid on a gunshot wound. In the distance, she heard faint sirens. *Thank goodness.*

* * *

Ronan Diamond looked up from today's newspaper to observe the smoke filtering over his fence from the adjacent yard.

The neighbor's grilling again. He shook his head. *Wonder how bad this time will be.*

During the month Ronan had lived there, he'd observed his neighbor attempting to grill on five different occasions. Snapping the newspaper back to reading level, he smirked at the volume of smoke rolling over the fence. The woman lacked the grilling gene.

Ronan didn't know his neighbor, but he'd admired her beauty and smokin' hot body the couple of times they'd nodded in passing. Neither seemed to keep normal eight-to-five work hours. He'd meant to introduce himself, but between his job as lieutenant at the local fire department and personally building his dream house on Amerine Lake, he was lucky to squeeze in five hours of sleep a night.

Hell. To be honest, he'd give up a few of those sleep hours for some commitment-free sex. At thirty-five, Ronan had had his share of girlfriends and lovers. When he'd gotten tired of being pushed toward marriage, he'd broken up with his last girlfriend. Sometimes the girl would do the dumping when she got tired of his work schedule. But either way, his relationships had all ended without a long-term commitment.

The grill smoke turned from gray to black and he wondered which takeout delivery service would be arriving tonight. His neighbor's pattern was to burn dinner and then order in.

Smelling the smoke and pondering restaurants made his stomach growl. Ronan was a respectable cook. His job demanded it. Even though he'd put the vast majority of his household stuff into storage while building his house, he refused to live without his Calphalon cookware and Wüsthof knives. He'd picked up a filet of sole and fresh asparagus for tonight's dinner. Since the fish needed about twenty minutes to bake, he pushed himself out of his chair and headed for his favorite room.

After turning on the oven to preheat, he pulled out the sole to prepare it. While he had the refrigerator open, he grabbed a beer, cracked the top, and took a long draw. The cold brew cooled his throat as it rolled toward his empty stomach.

He filled a double boiler to steam the asparagus, then oiled the pan for the fish. With a tilt of his head, he drained the rest of the beer and retrieved another. He downed half of it in one long gulp. When the beeper on the oven sounded, he finished his beer before putting in the fish to bake.

Body still, he sniffed. Something was burning. Not a burned food smell. Burning wood. He sniffed the air again. Moving into the dining room, he glanced out his French doors. Then he slammed them open. Orange-red flames ate the wooden fence at the rear property line. Black smoke churned into the sky. A large section of the fence collapsed with a loud roar.

"Aw, shit. Fire!" He snatched his cell and called 911 before racing outside for the hose curled at the side of the house. The fence was a total loss, but by using his hose he could keep the blaze from spreading.

The wail of sirens broke into the crackle of burning wood. His station would be the responders. He blew out a huff of exasperation. He'd never live this down.

Through the burned opening in the fence, Ronan eyed his grill-challenged neighbor holding a small kitchen pitcher. She wore a short, pink silk kimono that barely covered her crotch. Long, wet hair dripped down both sides of the robe, plastering the damp material to her full, lush body. When she turned to shush her barking dog, he got a nice view of the robe cupping the globes of her rear and an erect nipple saluting him through the now-almost-transparent material. His cock sat up and took notice of her bodacious body. He adjusted the crotch of his cargo shorts.

Throughout the twenty minutes involved for his guys to extinguish the fire and complete the fire report, his neighbor kept tugging at the robe as though pulling the edges closer would somehow maintain her modesty. Instead, each tug hiked up the hem a fraction of an inch. A few more and they'd all know if she was a natural blonde or not.

Bree looked at her grill lying in the mud by the fence. Its legs collapsed, wet coals spilled in the black, burned grass next to the remnants of the fence. Now that the guys were gone, she had to admit to being embarrassed—first, she'd started a fire that burned down a fire lieutenant's fence. Then she'd stood outside with a group of firemen in a short robe that stuck to her wet body like a second skin. She could have been naked and the men would have seen her body just as well.

"I hope you have insurance," a deep male voice said.

Her gaze jumped up from the mess in the grass into the angry grey eyes of her hunky neighbor. Not the way she'd planned on meeting him, but...

"I am so sorry," she said.

"I'm sure," he said.

At the harsh tone in his voice, she flinched. "Really. I am so sorry. I never dreamed something like that could happen. I thought I was being careful to get the hot coals away from my house."

He arched an eyebrow. "So you'd only burn down your neighbor's place?"

Heat flushed her cheeks. "I didn't mean to burn down your fence," she said defensively. When he didn't reply, she added,

"I'll make it up to you."

"Do you have insurance?"

"Yes, of course."

"Then it'll replace the fence, but that's not the current problem."

"Oh?"

"My dinner is now overcooked and ruined."

She cringed. "Please, let me do something to make up for this mess."

"Really? You want to make this up to me?"

"Oh yes. Please. Nothing would make me happier."

"Fine. You can replace my dinner. Tomorrow night. You cook at my house—wearing exactly what you have on right now."

Bree's heart skipped a beat. Her pussy throbbed. Arousal trickled down her thighs. "But..."

He gave a careless shrug and turned to leave. "So you weren't serious about making it up to me?" He took one step.

"Wait." Could this be happening? "It's just that..."

He turned and gave her that damned arched eyebrow again. "Take it or leave it, honey. Makes no difference to me."

Behind her navel, her gut tugged with interest. He got two steps away before she said, "Okay."

"Be at my back door by six tomorrow night." His gaze moved down, then up her body, eyes darkening with desire.

Heat and lust flared inside. Her nipples pushed against the silk. She forced herself to not cross one leg over the other to stem the tide of creamy fluid gushing from her sex. She felt stripped naked. And heaven help her if she didn't love it.

"And," he continued, "if you're wearing anything other than what we've agreed on, I won't answer the door and you can forget it."

As soon as his door shut, she hurried back to her townhouse

and into the shower for another date with her massager.

The next day, Ronan knocked off work early to pick up supplies for dinner, just in case his neighbor really did mean to cook. She'd shocked him yesterday when she'd agreed to his demand. His cock had grown so hard at the thought of seeing her in the silk robe and nothing else that he'd had to do most of his talking with his back toward her.

Maybe he should have made her come last night, while she was still feeling guilty about his fence. He could probably have gotten laid without much effort. But he wanted her at his control through choice, not guilt. If she showed up tonight, especially wearing nothing but her robe—and he was thinking that was probably a big if—she was taking the next step because she wanted to. He wanted her naked, spread-eagled, taking him deep—in her mouth and in her pussy. With that thought he grew painfully hard.

At six o'clock, a timid knock sounded at his patio door. He looked through the glass, saw the pink kimono robe, and unlocked the door for his guest. "You came," he said.

"I had a choice?"

"You always have a choice."

She stepped inside and held her arms out to her side. "Per your request."

He raised his finger in the air and twirled it around. She turned in a circle. When she faced him again, he nodded his approval, although he suspected she wore panties tonight, when she hadn't yesterday. He turned and walked into the kitchen, never checking to see if she was following. Her bare feet padded on his hardwood floor. He could smell her arousal. His body stiffened when her warm hand touched his shoulder.

"Am I really here to cook dinner?" Her voice was soft, almost shy. "I'm thinking I'm not."

His blood flowed from his brain to his dick. He turned to face her. "I'm not very hungry."

"I'm starved," she said. "But not for food." She stepped close and ran a hand down the front of his shorts.

His breath hissed.

Closing her fingers around his cock, she said, "These shorts might be cutting off your blood flow and we can't have that. Don't you agree?"

"I do."

She stopped him when he reached for the zipper. "Let me." She unfastened the button at his waist and lowered his zipper.

Dropping to her knees, she pulled down his shorts and leaned forward. Hot lips and breath caressed his straining flesh. He threaded his fingers into her hair to keep her face pressed to his shaft. Her long blond hair trailed down the sides of his calves. With her head bent, he couldn't see the action of her mouth, but he felt her teeth as she scraped down his cock. He drew in a sharp breath. Reaching down, he pulled her to her feet and took her mouth in a hot, violent kiss. A mesh of tongues and teeth. Neither ceding control.

The elastic of his briefs stretched away from his body. Her long fingers wrapped him in a silky embrace. His hips thrust against her palm.

He pulled his mouth away from hers, moving his lips and teeth across her cheek and down her throat. He ran his tongue into the dip at the base of her throat, then traced a path back up to her ear to run the tip around the rim.

She moaned and squeezed his cock. Her other hand joined her first to pull his briefs from his body and ease them over his straining penis. She didn't have to push far before he stepped from them, leaving them on the floor beside his shorts.

Jerking his T-shirt over his head, he tossed it on the pile and reached for the tie holding her robe. The silky material loosened easily. He shoved both hands onto her shoulders under the material and pushed the robe off. Underneath she wore only a thong.

"I told you to wear what you had on yesterday, and lady, you didn't have panties on. We can't have that." He reached into a drawer behind him and took out a sharp knife.

Her eyes rounded and she bit her lip.

Slipping his knife under the string at her hip, he sliced through. He repeated the motion on the other side. The scrap of lace stayed in place until she spread her legs; then it fluttered to the floor. "Better. Much better," he muttered, and put the knife back on the counter.

When he lifted her into his arms, she gasped in surprise. She wrapped her arms around his neck and pressed her mouth to his. Her tongue pushed its way into his mouth while he walked. When he stopped, she broke the kiss and looked around his living room. He let her legs slide to the thick rug.

"Get on your knees," he commanded in a voice thick with lust. When she didn't move fast enough, he added, "Now."

She lowered to her knees. The beating of her heart was a marching band in her ears. Her thighs were coated with her own thick cream. Heart pounding, she licked her lips and waited.

He sat on the sofa and spread his legs. "Come here."

She obeyed.

"Take me in your mouth."

Her fingers wrapped around his thickness and she ran her tongue along the slit at the end, savoring his salty juices. Lowering her head, she put her lips over the fat head and slid down his length.

He hissed. "Fuck," he muttered.

She almost smiled. Exactly what she had in mind.

The plump head hit the back of her throat and she adjusted to allow him to slide into her throat. His fingers threaded through her hair as he wrapped his hands around her head. He held tight, forcing more of his long dick down her throat. She pulled back slowly, allowing her teeth to scrape the engorged veins. Her fingers tightened around the base and followed her mouth up, then back down.

His breathing was choppy and rough. "Oh fuck," he groaned. "Deeper," he said with a thrust of his hips.

She took all he demanded. Slipping one hand between his legs, she cupped his balls, rolling them between her fingers. Smiling, she pulled off his dick and wrapped her lips around one ball, ran her tongue across it, and sucked hard.

His hips jerked. "Careful with the junk, honey," he cooed.

Bree continued to suck and fondle, moving her fingers to the area in front of his anus to stroke the soft skin there.

With a groan, he slid forward to give her better access.

She licked his balls and traced her tongue back up the under-side of his cock to the tip. After circling the head with her tongue, she took him deep into her mouth in one long slide, her fingers stroking the soft skin behind his balls. Her own juices tickled as they ran down her thigh. She pulled her hand from him and put it between her own legs. Her fingers separated her folds as she tried to give herself some relief.

Strong fingers wrapped around her wrist and pulled her hand away. "Bad girl," he said. "You're being punished for wearing panties. You can't touch yourself. You have to wait."

She pulled her mouth off his dick. "Bastard."

He laughed. "Oh hell yeah, I am." He grabbed her head and pushed her face back down to his crotch. "Now finish what you started." He stood, leaving her on her knees. "Open your mouth," he demanded. When she didn't, he grasped her hair and pulled her head back until their gazes met. "Open that beautiful fucking mouth, honey."

She smiled and separated her lips.

He drove his dick deep and pumped his hips. She sucked with all the force she could manage. His fingers made fists in her hair, pulling the strands taut from her head. She slid both hands up the soft skin between his thighs until she could cup his balls and stroke the area behind. She raked her nails across that sensitive skin, digging in just enough to be sharp but not painful.

"Damn, woman," he said in a huff of breath. "Damn."

His hip thrusts became faster and harder; she knew he was close.

"I'm about ten seconds from coming," he said with a hard slam. "You understand what I'm saying?"

If she didn't stop him, he would come into her mouth. She smiled and pressed the most sensitive spot behind his scrotum. He thrust one last time. Hot, salty liquid shot against the back of her throat. She swallowed and sucked his jerking cock as the stream of warm come finally slowed. With her tongue, she cleaned his flesh as he pulled from her mouth.

He dropped heavily back onto the sofa cushions. "Damn." His head dropped back onto a fluffy pillow and he threw his arm over his brow. "That was incredible." He breathed heavily. "Fucking incredible."

"Thank you," she said, sitting back on her heels.

"Oh no," he said with a grin. "Thank *you*." He patted the cushion beside him. "Come here."

With a sensuous glide, she climbed onto the couch. He wrapped the arm that'd been over his face around her shoulders.

She nuzzled his neck. "Now am I forgiven for burning down

your fence?"

"Honey, you can burn my fence down anytime."

She smiled into his neck. "I'm Bree, by the way."

Eyebrow raised, he looked at her. "Ronan."

"Nice to meet you, Ronan."

He laughed and pulled her into his lap. "Nothing like a good neighbor, don't you agree?"

FIRE HAZARD

M. Marie

When I first smelled the smoke, I glanced toward the sliding glass door. Even though our apartment building forbade barbeques, with summer finally here, I was used to catching the faint smell of prohibited hamburgers and forbidden hot dogs from my neighbors' balconies. The door was shut, though, and I saw no smoke in the air.

Assuming that the odor was coming from one of the units above or below me, I turned my attention back to the TV screen. Before the movie could pull my attention fully back in, however, the piercing cry of the fire alarm tore through my apartment. My pulse jumped into my throat and my eyes shot over to the armchair near the window. My cat, Brute—a moody, long-haired twenty-five-pound Maine Coon—had been curled up asleep on the hunter green chair for the past three hours, but now he was fully alert, a sentinel, with his grey ears perked toward the speaker near the front door.

Our eyes met for a second, and then Brute's ears flattened

against his head. The hackles rose along his back and in an instant he disappeared under the couch.

"*Oh shit.*"

Dropping to my knees, I pressed my face against the rug and glanced into the shadows under the sofa. A pair of narrow yellow eyes glared back. The alarm shrieked incessantly.

Above the shrill sound, doors opened and closed and hurried footsteps sounded in the hallway. Looking under the couch again, I tried to coax my pet out, but he was resistant. My unease mounted. The scent of smoke grew stronger now, and when I glanced toward the front door, my view seemed hazy. I hoped it was just shaken nerves blurring my vision and not accumulating smoke.

A new sound suddenly pierced the air: *sirens.* The sound was faint still, but grew louder as they drew near. I hurried to the balcony door. Sliding it open, I stepped out and leaned over the railing to look down. Twenty floors below me, the sidewalk was in chaos as the residents of my building anxiously spilled out of the emergency stairwells onto the street. They lingered just outside the front entrance, clutching each other or what small items they had thought to grab before evacuating. I couldn't see their faces, but their movements and body language spoke of their confusion and alarm.

The sirens still approached.

My gaze shifted to the end of the block, where it intersected with Yonge Street. Traffic was always steady along this main downtown road, but at the moment it was dead. Not a single vehicle moved along Wood Street in either direction. The reason revealed itself in an instant: a long red fire engine cut through the oncoming lane and pulled onto our street with its lights flashing. A second fire engine followed, as well as one of the small trucks from the firehouse. As the caravan of emergency vehicles pulled to a stop outside our building, the crowd below surged into the parking lot across the street and the sidewalk began to fill with firefighters.

My heart leapt into my throat, and I quickly dashed back into my apartment. After sliding the door shut behind me, I hurried into the front hallway and threw open the coat closet. In the bottom left corner, under a rolled-up sleeping bag and the spare vacuum filters, was the cat carrier. I pulled the large green container out of the closet, ignoring the rest of the clutter as it spilled out across the floor, and hurried back into the living room.

Dropping to my knees in front of the couch again, I pressed my cheek against the area rug and searched the shadows for the familiar shape of my cat. It took a moment, but I finally spotted the nervous animal.

"Here, baby. Come out now, please," I called hopefully, extending my fingers towards him. I felt Brute press his nose against the tip of my middle finger for an instant, but then he pulled away. My impatience flared.

Cursing under my breath, I flattened my chest against the rug and extended my arm as far as I could. I felt my hand brush against soft fur, closed my grip around what I hoped was a hind leg, and pulled. An outraged hiss filled the small space, audible even over the continuous shriek of the fire alarm, and I quickly dragged the overweight cat out from under the couch. As soon as I pulled him free, he turned in my grasp and began to claw at my forearm.

"Ow! Quit it, Brute!" I yelped. Pulling myself up into a kneeling position, I shifted my grip to the ruff at the back of his neck and pressed him against my chest with one hand, then used my free hand to pull the cat carrier closer. Brute's furious struggling escalated as soon as he noticed the crate. His claws and teeth lashed against my arms, chest and thighs, but I refused to let him go. As soon as the crate was close enough, I opened the door and pushed him forward. I managed to get his head through the opening, but his paws immediately shot out and braced themselves against the rim. I tried to push him forward, but the stubborn animal pushed back.

The siren outside was still wailing in chaotic harmony with the screaming alarm system inside. I didn't have time to fight with my cat. I needed to get us *out*.

It was time to try another tactic.

Retracting the cat into the crook of my arm again, I tipped the carrier onto its end so that the opening was at the very top. I leaned forward, gripped Brute under his front legs, and held him above the cat crate, lining up his dangling back legs with that small opening, and dropped him. The shock of being released distracted him from what was below. He fell right through the doorway and into the cage without a protest, and I pounced on the door to fasten it shut before he could try to spring back out.

There was a moment of stunned silence, and I took advantage of my cat's confusion to jump to my feet, heft his cage up, and dash for the front door. Stepping out into the twentieth-floor hallway, I was terrified by the light grey smoke filling the air. For a moment I thought of retreating into my apartment, but resisted the fearful impulse.

I stepped out of my apartment door and squinted up and down the hallway. The smoke seemed thickest near the entrance of the garbage-chute room. I gripped Brute's heavy carrier with both hands and headed quickly for the staircase at the other end of the hall. The door was slightly ajar; I shouldered it opened and began my hasty descent.

The air was noticeably clearer in the stairwell. Brute, who had been uncharacteristically silent in the upstairs hallway, seemed to be reviving now that the air tasted less acrid. As I reached the landing for the seventeenth floor and hurried toward the next flight of stairs, he began to howl.

Brute's deep caterwauls filled the stairwell, echoing angrily from the penthouse to the basement. I was almost grateful for our delayed evacuation; the staircase was deserted. No one else had to witness my awkward descent with my verbally abusive companion. His volume escalated with each step, masking the frantic slapping of my feet as I dashed down the steps, as well as my panting and cursing as I struggled to hold his carrier steady.

Inside, he had begun shifting from side to side, trying to look out at his surroundings. His random movements made it difficult to prevent shaking the heavy carrier as I raced down the steps. Already, with his size and weight, I needed both hands to lift the cage. My balance, as I turned the corners and ran down the stairs, was precarious, but my surging adrenaline was doing a great job of keeping my thoughts away from the strong likelihood that I might trip and tumble down the concrete steps at any given moment.

With relief, I finally reached the bottom of the stairs. Pausing for a moment to catch my breath and readjust my grip on Brute's carrier, I shoved my hip against the heavy door and pushed it open.

The door led into the maintenance and storage area of the apartment building. Against the walls leaned snow shovels, bags of salt for the sidewalk, and rolled-up hoses. To the left was a door leading to the ramp entrance for the underground parking garage. To the right was the garbage room, where the garbage and recycling chutes emptied into their sorting bins. Clustered between all these doors were a least a dozen firefighters. As the door slammed shut behind me and Brute erupted in a new cacophony of complaints, every single one of those helmeted heads turned toward me.

I opened my mouth to speak—without having *any idea* what to say—but wasn't given the chance. Instantly, a ring formed around me and a volley of concerned questions filled the room.

"Are you all right, miss?"

"Are you hurt?"

"Do you need help?"

"What's in the cage?" The last question drew my attention to a middle-aged man standing to my left. His head was tilted toward the carrier and a hint of an amused smile was visible under the eye shield of his mask.

I frowned and shifted the carrier to my other hand. "My cat."

"Ahhh." He was grinning openly now. "He doesn't sound very happy. Did he give you all those cuts?"

Glancing down, I took notice of my appearance for the first time. It was Saturday morning and, although it was past eleven, I was still wearing my pajamas. The striped cotton sleep shorts barely reached my upper thighs and rode low on my hips. The matching pink camisole stretched just past my navel, but left a good inch of skin exposed between the hem of my top and the waistband of my shorts. Plain white athletic socks covered my feet, their bottoms a filthy grey from my run down the stairs. No one's attention seemed focused on my attire, though.

All eyes were on the blood.

Dried blood stained the front of my tank top. Above the neckline of the top, numerous scratch marks cut into my chest. They weren't deep, but more than one was still bleeding slug-gishly. Both forearms sported matching injuries, and the tops of my thighs were cut as well. No wonder my appearance had caused such a scene.

Feeling a warm flush spread over my face, I self-consciously tugged at the hem of my shirt and mumbled, "He was just upset by the noise and the carrier. I'm fine."

"Well, the alarm shouldn't be bothering him much longer," the smiling firefighter offered. "We've already contained the fire in the garbage room, and we'll be letting people re-enter the building shortly. I'm afraid it'll be a while before we get the elevators back up and running."

I felt a relieved smile spread across my face. "That's great! I'm not looking forward to carrying him back upstairs, though."

A larger man stepped forward from the back of the group and singled out the man beside me. "Jackson, why don't you help her back up to her apartment? Make sure she's all right. Sebastian is working on the alarm, and we have everything else here under control."

Jackson nodded. "No problem," he said as he stepped beside me. He reached down to touch his fingers to the handle of Brute's carrier. "May I?"

Gratefully, I allowed him to take my burden, then fell into step behind him. He held the door open for me, then took the lead as we started up the steps.

"What floor are we headed to?" he asked as we began our ascent.

"Twenty."

Jackson grunted and tightened his grip on the carrier. After a few minutes of climbing, the alarm stopped at last. The sudden silence rang in my ears, but the peaceful quiet was short-lived. Brute quickly filled the silence with his own penetrating cries.

Jackson paused on the next landing and tapped a gloved finger against the front bars of the carrier. "Calm down, buddy. We're almost there," he coaxed in a gentle, patient voice, before glancing back at me. "How about you? Holding up okay?"

His concerned expression made my face feel hot. Flustered, I nodded and hurried past him up the stairs.

We were both tired and breathing heavily when we finally reached the twentieth floor. I unlocked my door and held it open for the firefighter, then followed him inside. He stopped in the entryway and lowered the carrier to the floor. Straightening, he reached up and removed his helmet.

He wasn't quite as old as I had thought. His face was rugged, with dark, coarse stubble spread across his chin and jaw, but his blue eyes were bright. He grinned and I was reminded of a teasing teenager.

"Should I release the beast?" He gestured at Brute's cage.

I laughed. "Give me a minute to get out of the way! He's going to be mad." I backed into the washroom, then nodded. As soon as the man released the latch and opened the door, Brute shot out of the carrier with a fierce hiss and disappeared into the living room.

Jackson chuckled as he joined me. "Mission accomplished with no casualties," he joked, before a more serious expression crossed his face. "How about I look after you now?"

"Me?" Following his line of vision, I looked down at my injured arms. "Oh, you don't need to bother with me. I'll be fine."

Ignoring my weak protest, Jackson moved past me into the room and opened the medicine cabinet. As he began pulling down the supplies he needed, he gestured toward the counter. "Have a seat."

Uncertainly, I perched on the edge of the counter and watched as he removed his gloves and coat. He began by washing my arms with a damp facecloth. His touch was gentle, warm, and much softer than I had expected. The intense focus and care he put into the simple action of cleaning my wounds made my face flush and my heart beat rapidly.

Once the dried blood was washed away, he applied an anti-septic. I hissed at the sting and his deep chuckle filled the small room.

"Do you need me to blow on it?"

Blushing, I looked away from his teasing smile.

Next he moved his attention to my legs. The feel of his hands on my bare thighs made my breath catch in my throat. His touch was professional, and yet it seemed to linger longer than neces-sary as he treated the cuts in my pale flesh.

He was standing quite close; I could feel the heat of his large body against my thighs, which were spread to either side of him. Another steady heat was beginning to grow between my legs and spread throughout my body—an insistent, demanding heat that was making my pulse hammer and my pussy swell.

If he came any closer, I was certain he would feel it.

As his hand began to move towards the scratch mark on my inner thigh, I reached down to grasp it in alarm. He glanced up and our eyes met. Something in my eyes must have betrayed my dilemma. That teasing grin returned—and although his captured hand lay still, his free hand now began to rove across my other bare thigh, toward my hip.

"Are you not feeling well?" he asked kindly, but his eyes were shining with mischief.

I swallowed back the moan that his exploring touch had evoked, and shook my head. "I'm fine," I replied softly, as I released my grip on his hand.

He immediately returned his focus to the final scratch on my leg. He folded back the inner hem of my shorts to expose the area, then reached for the facecloth. My pussy grew wetter with each pass of the damp cloth. More than once, his knuckles brushed against my soft mound, and it was all I could do not to moan for more.

Before applying the antiseptic, he placed his left hand on my hip to brace me as the wet cotton ball came into contact with my irritated skin.

I surprised us both when I suddenly said, "Blow on it."

He looked up at me quickly, then lowered his face close to my crotch. His breath was cool against my thigh, but it ignited an immediate fire in my loins. I spread my legs wider and lifted my hips slightly.

He blew again. This time he turned his face as he did so, letting his breath spread inward, away from my cut and toward my cunt.

I was breathless. I spread my legs even wider, but was disappointed when he straightened again. He quickly rekindled my arousal, though, when his gaze fell on my heaving chest. "Just one more area to treat."

My hands fell to the hem on my camisole. With more bravado than I had ever imagined I possessed, I lifted the garment over my head and let it fall to the floor. His glance moved over my chest, taking in the shallow cuts first, and then moving on to my flat stomach, small firm breasts, and stiff nipples.

Despite the hard erection I could feel through his overalls as he leaned into me, Jackson took his time caring for my cuts first. With the same careful attention his hand had shown my arms and thighs, he bathed my upper chest, then gently dried it before reaching for the dreaded antiseptic. This time he didn't wait for an invitation.

Even before I had finished hissing, Jackson's breath was on my bare skin. He blew across my chest, then against the sensitive skin in the shallow valley between my breasts, before his breath ghosted over my left nipple.

The already-stiff peak hardened further and I let a sweet moan escape my lips. Reaching back, I braced both hands on the cool countertop behind me and arched my back, presenting my chest to Jackson.

His lips closed around my rosebud nipple immediately, sucking hard. His hands gripped my hips tightly and I wrapped my legs around his waist, pressing my body close. The heat at my center burned hot now.

I ground our groins together and with a grunt Jackson tightened his grip and lifted me off the counter. His lips moved to my neck and his hands slid up my back. I wrapped my arms around his neck.

Spinning around, he leaned back against the counter, settled me on his hips, and let his hands rove lower. They cupped my backside, squeezing, before one hand slid lower. I felt his fingers push the leg of my shorts aside, then breach the elastic hem of my panties.

My pussy was wet and waiting for him. His index finger slipped easily between the damp lips of my opening. I moaned as his middle finger quickly joined the first and both fingers began moving. He stroked my inner lips from back to front; the unusual angle of penetration intensified my arousal. My nerve endings danced under his touch as he inched his way slowly toward my clit.

His mouth found my chest again. While his fingers stroked my inner folds, his lips trailed soft kisses across the space between my breasts before reaching the peak of my right nipple. Pulling it into his mouth, his tongue circled the hard nub, flicking at the tip while his lips applied pressure to the point of contact. He broke the kiss, pulled back, and blew on the now-moist rosebud. The coolness of his breath after the heat of his open-mouthed kiss made me shudder. It was sensual torture.

With another boyish grin, he moved for the other nipple while his fingers finally reached my clitoris. They circled my pearl, pinching it gently between them. I moaned and begged for more. His blunt fingernail dragged across the sensitive nub, and the washroom echoed with my cries as I trembled on the edge of orgasm.

I was so desperately close.

His walkie suddenly crackled to life and a distorted voice called out, "Jackson? We're done here. You on your way?"

Jackson looked at me. In his dark blue eyes I could see that leaving was the last thing he wanted to do. Still, he was on duty. Withdrawing his fingers, he lowered me carefully to the ground and retrieved the communicating device. With an apologetic expression, he lifted the walkie to his ear. "Be right down," he sighed into the mouthpiece, before collecting his discarded clothing.

I followed him out into the hallway.

"My shift ends in two hours," he said over his shoulder as he reached for the doorknob.

Brute suddenly darted out from under the bench beside the door and dashed between Jackson's legs. The sudden movement startled the man, and he stumbled forward, hitting the door.

"Are you ok?" I gasped, rushing forward, but my concern faded as Jackson's deep laughter filled the apartment.

"That cat is a fire hazard!" he teased, grinning broadly, before pulling me forward for a kiss so deep I felt my heart rise up in my chest. Pulling back, he repeated his earlier suggestion. "See you in two hours?"

"You know where to find *us*," I replied, grinning, as Brute wound around my ankles, purring.

THE FIREMAN'S RESCUE

Kalissa Wayne

D rew really didn't need the extra stress at work. Being fire chief was stressful enough, but he'd been dealing with an aggravating new employee for the past three months.

True, the sheriff also had to deal with her, but his best friend Jonas Quinn seemed to get along fine with the new dispatcher, Heather Titsworth.

Drew snorted. *Titsworth.* What kind of name was that? If he'd been a woman with that last name, he'd have legally changed it as soon as he'd turned eighteen.

He stopped at the one red light in town and sighed as he looked around the intersection, noting how few windows were bright. The combination police station/firehouse/dispatch center was the only building in the downtown area still lit up.

Glancing at the time, he realized that Heather would be off work by now. The meeting had ended on time, but council members had wanted to talk to him about his hair. Again. He refused to cut his hair just because they thought it didn't look professional. It was his one vanity and a last remnant of his heritage, a deep bluish-black that reached to his waist and had never been cut.

Drew smirked. It didn't hurt that women loved his hair. Women had always fallen all over themselves vying for his attention. *Until her.* Drew glared at the station.

What was it about her that irritated him? Was it because she didn't fawn over him? But why wouldn't she? She wasn't beautiful. "Just Call Me Heather" Titsworth was about five foot eight and chunky, wore glasses, and had plain brown hair pulled back into an even plainer ponytail. He couldn't even remember if her eyes were green or blue. Unremarkable in every way.

Although just this morning, when he had walked in the door connecting the firehouse to the dispatch center, he'd gotten quite an eyeful as she stretched across her desk to hand one of the deputies some paperwork. Heather had been wearing her usual baggy jeans and overly large shirt, but when she reached out, her jeans had hugged her ass and her shirt had ridden up.

Three things had shocked Drew: those jeans were hugging a beautiful ass; she had a tattoo; and he'd wanted to lick it. Across the small of Heather's back was a pair of Celtic angel wings. "Just Call Me Heather" had a tramp stamp, and he'd gotten as hard as a steel bat looking at it.

"You going to sit here all night blocking traffic, or do I need to give you a ticket?" Jonas pulled up next to him, chuckling. "Still stewing over the council's hair phobia?" Jonas was also full-blooded Native American, his black hair every bit as long as Drew's. Jonas also refused to cut his hair.

"Nah. They can go jump in the lake about my hair. I was just sitting here trying to figure out some problems. As for blocking traffic..." Drew looked around. The sheriff's truck and his were the only two vehicles on the road. "I don't think I'll block traffic until about six-thirty in the morning."

"Come on back to the station and I'll buy you a cup of—" Jonas was interrupted when the radio crackled.

"Calling all officers. House fire reported at 902 New York Street. Possible trapped residents. Freddie, that's the Gueterbergs' house! Hey, calling all officers. *House fire at the Gueterbergs'.*"

Both men flipped on their lights and sirens and headed toward the residence. Lights flicked on in the houses as they passed. The volunteers would be there shortly, and the one sleeping at the station that night would drive the truck there ASAP.

As they pulled up in front of the house, fire engulfed the roof. The elderly Mr. Gueterberg sat in the yard in his wheelchair. Mrs. Gueterberg stood beside him, holding his oxygen mask to his face.

Drew quickly suited up.

"Oh, thank God!" Mrs. Gueterberg cried as they rushed up. "You have to help her! She went back in to save Johnnie. She's been in there a long time. She helped us get out, but when Günter told her Johnnie was still inside, she rushed back in. She doesn't—"

Drew had heard enough; he ran up the steps into the house. Fire raged in the living room. He heard coughing from the back of the house and quickly ran that way. Through the smoke, he saw someone trying to open the door to a back room. Just as he yelled through his mask to tell the woman to get out, he heard the roof above him groan. Glancing upward, he saw flames licking across the stucco. A second later, a large beam crashed through. He leapt to the side, but caught a blow to the side of his head and crumpled to the floor.

* * *

Disoriented and coughing, Heather heard someone yelling right before a beam fell through the ceiling. Thank God. She'd been ready to give up searching because the fire was getting out of hand and she could barely breathe, even hunched close to the floor.

Blinking to clear the tears from her smoke-filled eyes, she saw a pair of feet lying beneath a pile of burning rubble next to a table. She edged around the burning beam that had landed partially on the table, and knelt beside the large pair of feet.

This had to be Johnnie. She grabbed his ankles and dragged him toward the back door. They had to get out now.

Flinging the back door wide open, she grabbed the ankles again and used all her strength to pull the big man out. He weighed a ton; between her eyes streaming from the smoke and coughing her head off, she was quickly losing steam.

She backed out onto the porch, but stumbled when she unexpectedly found the steps, twisting her ankle. Still holding onto the man, she screamed as she fell backward and dragged the poor man with her.

At the bottom, she wiped her eyes to clear them. The man— not Johnnie, because he wore a fireman's gear—lay half on the porch and halfway down the stairs. She gazed up. The porch roof and supports were ablaze.

Struggling to rise, she grabbed a wrist and pulled, rolling him down the stairs and on top of her, knocking the breath out of her. With darkness enveloping her, the last thing she saw were three men rolling the fireman away and hands reaching down to pull her away from the porch as it collapsed.

A stinging pain at his left temple jerked Drew awake. Two pairs of hands held him down.

"Hey, relax, tiger. You're still among the living. Just breathe." An oxygen mask was forced over his nose and mouth as Jonas's voice spoke to him.

Drew's eyes were still blurry, so he couldn't see who was who. In the background he heard the sounds of the fire crew working to put out the blaze. Blinking to regain focus, he realized Jonas was holding the mask while a volunteer EMT cleaned his face. He lay on the grass in the Gueterbergs' front lawn. Just great.

Reaching up, he waved the EMT towards the fire.

Jonas pressed his hand to the mask. "Hold that." Then he finished cleaning the side of Drew's face. "You know, I almost had a heart attack when you ran in that house. Just after you disappeared, a big flame shot out the doorway and blocked the exit. Lucky for you, someone dragged your sorry ass out the back door."

"Who..." Drew tried to ask, but started coughing.

"Don't try to talk. Everyone got out fine. They're taking the Gueterbergs to the hospital, just for observation. You appear to have gotten the worst of it. What did you hit your head on, anyway? You've been out almost a couple of minutes. Best get you to the hospital, too."

Drew cleared his throat and coughed again. "Just take me to the station. The night dispatcher...can keep an eye on me...if you feel I need to be watched." Drew's voice was gravelly, but at last the coughing subsided.

As Jonas pulled a bandage out and applied it to his head, he said, "Sounds like a plan. I know your hard head." Jonas reached down and offered Drew a hand to sit up.

Drew knelt for a moment until his head stopped spinning, then pushed up to his feet to watch as his crew fought the blaze. The house would be a total loss. All his men could do was keep the fire contained until it burned itself out.

Glancing to the side, he noted two more EMTs stood near the back of a pickup parked at the curb, but he couldn't see who they were talking to.

Moving toward the truck and the EMTs, he felt a chill as he saw a bent head, the top of which looked very familiar. Anger and fear shot up his spine and his temper exploded. "What the hell were you doing in that house?" He shoved his way between his men, not caring that his voice was loud and hoarse. "Do you realize you could still be trapped in there, burning to death, putting others in danger, all because of a stupid cat?"

Heather lifted her head, and he got his first glimpse of her soot-smudged cheeks. Her tears had traced clean tracks down her cheeks. Her reddened eyes were glistening pools of turquoise. More tears welled. "I didn't know..."

"Don't think your tears are going to save you. I should fire you right now for this stupid little stunt."

"Boss, don't..."

"Drew, she didn't..."

Both of the EMTs tried to interrupt Drew, but he glared them into silence. He turned back to see Heather hop off the tailgate of the truck.

"You can't fire me for trying to help," she said, raising her chin. "I did what anyone would have done. When I saw the fire, I called it in, then ran inside to check for residents. Mrs. Gueterberg wouldn't leave her husband, so I got him into his wheelchair and she led the way out of the house. She went down the steps and I took him down the ramp. He was upset and told me Johnnie was still inside, so once I got them far enough from the house, I went back in. I didn't know it was a damned cat, otherwise I would have lied and told them I saw it outside." She shoved Drew hard in the chest, stormed around the truck, climbed in, and took off.

Drew stood speechless. He turned and saw all three men, Jonas and the two EMTs, standing with arms crossed over their chests and glaring at him. "What? She shouldn't have been in there."

The EMTs threw him disgusted looks and went to help with the hoses. Jonas continued to glare.

"What? You know she shouldn't have been in there!"

Jonas shook his head. "You've had your ass in a knot ever since she came to town. Why? She's a sweet lady who'd do anything for anyone and never ask for a thank you. Think about this: she was doing exactly what you would have done." As Jonas turned to walk away, he added over his shoulder, "And on top of that, she saved your sorry ass."

Drew threw his hands into the air and looked around for his second-in-command. Chester Short stood by the truck talking to a couple of the neighbors. Drew checked in with him, decided things were under control, and told him he was heading to the station to clean up.

An hour later, halfway through a shower, Drew was still fuming. He was angry Heather had walked away, angry she had even been in the house in the first place, and angry with himself for reasons he couldn't explain. Her eyes haunted him.

Some emotion burned inside his chest; he didn't want to admit what he'd been feeling ever since the day he'd walked into the office to help Jonas interview her. Whatever it was gave him a raging hard-on.

Nothing about her would attract a man at first glance, and yet he'd felt lust grip his balls the moment they'd been introduced. Every day since then, when he'd walked into the station to see her laughing and cutting up with the other men, something had twisted in his chest, making him grouchy for the rest of the day.

Right now his chest felt tight and ready to explode. He had to see her, had to know if she was all right, had to check her over himself. Drew braced an arm against the shower wall and fought to bring his emotions into some semblance of order. The hot water turned ice cold, but even that didn't affect his out-of-control cock.

Drew sent it a disgusted look, turned off the water, and decided he needed to go check on "Just Call Me Heather." Strictly a professional call. Strictly. Right.

"Oh hell. Who am I kidding?" Drew asked himself as he forced his stiff cock into a pair of jeans.

After ringing the doorbell to no avail, Drew hammered her front door. "Heather? Answer me, girl, or I'm going to break down the door." Drew resumed his heavy pounding.

The door swung open. Drew paused mid-knock, his fist near his ear.

"Girl? Really?" Heather pulled the tie on her robe tight and gave him a hard look, as if he were insane.

Drew didn't move a muscle. Where was the plain girl from work? Heather's hair was out of its ponytail, falling just past her shoulders in waves, slightly mussed as if she'd been asleep. Her face was tinged pink, her eyes soft and drowsy.

The robe she wore was old and threadbare. His breath had stopped the minute she'd pulled the door open. The light from inside outlined her body through the thin material, and what he was seeing was downright awe-inspiring.

He slowly lowered his hand and walked forward, crowding her back into the cabin. Once inside, he pulled the door out of her hand, closed it, and flipped the deadbolt, never once breaking eye contact.

"Drew? What's wrong?" she asked in a sleep-husky voice.

But he just kept crowding her, and she shuffled backwards, limping, until her hips hit the sofa arm.

Drew grabbed her arms to steady her. "Heather, are you all right? Did you get hurt earlier? I need to be sure." His voice was still a touch gravelly, but whether it was from the smoke or something else, he didn't know.

"I'm fine. Um, nothing a couple more ibuprofen and sleep won't cure," Heather said, distractedly. Her gaze was focused on his chest.

Drew ran his hands up her arms, then slid them behind her shoulders and knees and picked her up.

For a second, she held still, then bucked in his arms. "What the hell are you doing? Put me down!"

Turning, he walked around the fireplace wall and sat her on the edge of her brass bed. Kneeling at her feet, he parted the robe and lifted first her right foot, then her left. Muttering curses under his breath, he gently held her injured left foot and probed the swollen area.

At her hiss, he looked up and apologized. "I'm sorry. I just wanted to make sure you were okay. I didn't mean to cause you pain. Is there anywhere else you're hurt?" He propped her foot on his thigh as he ran his hands slowly up her calves to her knees, pushing the robe open as he went.

Trying to keep the robe closed against his marauding hands, Heather said "Drew, I'm fine. I told you I only have some minor injuries. They've already been looked at by the EMTs."

Drew's eyes were on her knees. He leaned down and kissed the faint bruise on her left knee, closing his eyes as he ran his tongue gently around its edges.

Her breath caught, but he ignored the sound and let his hands travel up her silky thighs, pushing the robe further open. Heather tried to keep her modesty intact by grabbing the material over her mound and holding it closed, but he was more insistent. A faint trail of bruises flowed from her knee to her upper thigh and disappeared under the robe.

Drew lowered his head and continued trailing kisses and licks up her thigh until he reached the material. Then, forcing her knees apart, he knelt between them, laid his head in her lap, and wrapped his arms around her.

"Drew? Are you okay?" Heather tentatively placed a hand on his hair and stroked his head, running her fingers through his loose hair.

He shook his head, but tightened his arms around her. "I could have lost you today," he blurted. "My stubborn pride wouldn't listen to my heart. I almost lost you before I could tell you." He paused, took a deep breath, and squeezed her tighter, not looking up. He felt foolish enough after everything he'd done—bawling her out at the fire and pounding on her door like a lunatic—but he was desperate to tell her everything and didn't want her to stop him before he was done. "I... I have feelings for you, Heather," he said, his voice thick. "I've fought them since the day you walked into the station, but I can't ignore them anymore. I can't take the chance I'll lose you before we explore what this could be." Lifting his head, he met her wide gaze. "Question is, what do you feel?"

Eyes blue as turquoise were wide and round. She swallowed hard. "Oh, Drew. I've had...mixed emotions about you since day one. Sometimes I lo...like you, sometimes I could kick your ass. And I was upset I almost got us both killed over a cat." Her lips twitched at the corners. "But you did piss me off when you threatened to fire me."

"Sorry about that. I was just so shaken up about you being in the middle of the danger. I never would have fired you." Drew turned his head down and nuzzled into the crevice between

Heather's thighs. Reaching a hand around, he untied the robe's belt and flipped the robe open. Drawing in a deep breath, he growled, "You smell so damn good. I could feast here all night." With those words, he gripped the sides of her bikini panties and ripped them off her.

"Drew! What are you...ahhh!"

Heather stopped mid-sentence as Drew's mouth made contact with her slit. His hands pushed her thighs wider, then one slid up her stomach to push her down on the bed. Wrapping his arms under her thighs, he propped her legs over his shoulders and pulled her bottom to the edge of the bed, leaving her open and vulnerable to his invading mouth. His tongue ran laps up and down her drenched folds, circling her clit and her opening before his thumb brushed her clit and she jerked.

"Easy, baby. My control is shaky. Right now, all I want to do is pound into you and screw you for days. Let me make you come this way, then we'll see where we go from there." Heather's answer was a soft moan and fingers clenching in his hair. He grinned as he placed a soft kiss on the thigh next to his cheek, and then dove in for more of her sweet honey.

With his thumb circling closer and closer to her swollen clit, brushing it every now and then, his mouth worked the soft folds of her pussy. Kissing, licking, and nibbling gently, he thrust his tongue in deep to draw more honey to the surface. As her body tightened and her pussy tried to clench on his tongue, he rubbed harder with his thumb.

Drew thrust a finger from his free hand into her pussy and pumped, while his lips closed around her clit and sucked. She buried her fingers in his hair, clamped her thighs around his head, and screamed as an orgasm overtook her.

He grabbed her thighs and pried them open to lick her honey until she had recovered. As he felt the tension begin to build in her again, he placed a kiss at the top of her mound and stood. He stripped off his clothes, then gently removed the robe from her arms and moved her into the center of the bed.

She looked like an angel, one he wanted beyond all else. He had gotten even harder listening to her cry out in ecstasy as he made her come. His control was better now, though; he wouldn't finish on the first stroke.

He crawled slowly onto the bed and ran his hands between her legs to spread her open again. Her pussy glistened with her honey. Levering her legs over his arms, he knelt between her thighs and pulled her toward him until his cock lay along her slit, wallowing in her moisture. He drew a deep breath between his closed teeth.

"Drew, there's something you should know. It... It's been quite a while for me." She lowered her eyes and blushed. "I'm not sure if I can please you..."

"Heather, look at me." When she still averted her eyes, he tapped her butt. She jumped and looked up at him in shock. "Heather. You are beautiful. I want you more every day. I'll take it slow, and I'll try to be gentle. If I hurt you, let me know and I'll stop."

Then, placing the crown of his cock at her entrance, he pushed inside.

She was so tight around his cock, he wasn't sure if he could last. She felt virgin-tight. Slowly rocking against her, he fed her his cock an inch at a time until she became accustomed to his large length and girth. She felt like the sweetest of vices around his aching cock.

As he sank the last inch in, seating it to the hilt inside her silky grip, he paused and clenched his jaw to keep from going off. She was so perfect. Why had he fought this for so long? Repositioning his grip on her legs, he looked down at her face.

Her eyes were glazed, her face flushed with passion, and he couldn't wait to fuck her raw. "Baby? I don't know if I can be as gentle as I should be, but I'll try."

"Drew, don't hold back. I want to feel you. I feel like I'm filled to overflowing, but it's going to feel so good when you make love to me. Please, Drew, give me all you got."

And that broke what little control Drew had. He pulled out, then powered back in one stroke. Hearing her moan turned him on. He wanted to hear more.

He stroked slow and easy at first, then increased his speed. Her sweet, hot pussy clamped down on him. Her breaths turned to pants, interlaced with keening moans.

She gasped his name and reached for him, but her position made it impossible to do anything but caress his chest. Her fingernails were short, but as he drove harder into her she scratched his chest, leaving ragged trails on his skin. The sight created a bonfire in his balls.

Drew pounded into her. The bedsprings squeaked and the headboard hit the wall, adding to their symphony of sexual sounds—the hot, liquid squish of her pussy as he powered in and out, the slapping of flesh as his hips hit hers, his balls banging her ass. She moaned and whimpered, trying to keep from screaming. He wasn't having it.

"Come on, baby. Let it out," he crooned. "If you feel like screaming, scream. That's it baby. Does my cock pounding into you make you hot? Does the thought of us doing this for hours sound good? Ah, baby. I could keep this up all night, you feel so good." Drew threw his head back as he felt Heather's pussy clamp down at his words.

"One day, real soon, we'll spend the day in bed and see how much fucking we can handle. I want to take you like this again. I want to see you spread out over the end of the bed, clawing at the blankets as I pound you from behind. I'll grab your hips to hold you still. You'd like that, wouldn't you?" He knew she would. Her eyelids drifted down and she clenched harder on his cock.

"Or maybe, one day, I'll call you into my office and lock the door. I'll pull those baggy pants of yours down, then run my hands up under your shirt, grab these beautiful breasts, and bend you over my desk." Her eyes widened, so he smiled. "But you'd have to be quiet there. After all, good girls don't fuck the boss at work."

She screamed at that one and another orgasm began to shudder through her. Wow. He'd have to make note of that.

Right now, she arched up, shuddering and creaming all over his cock. He groaned at the hot flood of her honey around his shaft, dripping down onto his balls. Her hands gripped his forearms, fingernails clenching into his skin. That small bite of pain sent his senses reeling. She was so hot, so tight. He felt a third orgasm shaking her body as he continued to pound into her.

Leaning forward, he wrapped his arms around her, buried his face in her neck, felt the electricity pour down his spine and gather in his balls. One final thrust and he stayed deep as his orgasm exploded, hot jets of semen splashing into her while her fourth orgasm milked his cock. Her nails raked his back, causing him to arch like a cat into the feeling. He continued to hump into her until the last quiver of both their orgasms had faded.

Kissing her neck, he ran his hands over her shoulders and down to her breasts. He didn't have the strength to move just yet. He rubbed the outer curve of her breast. "I'm sorry, Heather," he growled against her skin. "I didn't mean to be so rough. Or so abrupt. I never even got to pay attention to these lovely ladies. Can you forgive me?"

Her breath caught on a gasp. "Only if you do that again, real soon."

"So, Heather," he mumbled against her breast, "how about our first date tomorrow night? We can see where this relationship is headed."

"I'd like that. Though I think we got a few things out of order, let's see where this will lead. On one condition."

He raised his head to look at her. She was blushing.

"When you call me in your office, I want you in your uniform and suspenders. I think you look hot in those suspenders."

And as the sun came up, the sounds of bedsprings squeaking, a headboard banging, and beautiful moaning could still be heard.

FALLING ASHES

Shoshanna Evers

S usan couldn't bring herself to turn off the television, even
though the reporter standing in front of the forest fire on her
screen kept repeating the same things over and over: The firefighters were working around the clock to extinguish the fire.
An evacuation route had been set up but no one lived in that
part of the woods...

Thank God.

At least five firefighters had been airlifted out by the med-
evac team for treatment of burns and smoke inhalation...

She swallowed the bile rising in her throat and refused to
cry. But she couldn't seem to turn off the damn TV. None of the
surrounding fire stations were even answering the phone, which
wasn't exactly a shocker since every other wife and girlfriend
and—whatever she was to Trent—was probably calling around
in a panic, just like she'd been doing.

What if Trent was hurt? He'd started his shift almost twenty-
four hours ago; surely they'd relieve him soon so another round

of firefighters could go in. But what if he was one of the guys who'd been helicoptered out to the hospital?

Her cabin was miles from the fire, miles past the evacuation line, even, but still she could smell the smoke of thousands of trees burning. Tiny white ashes fluttered down past her windows like a light snow.

Trent, where are you?

Her cell phone remained silent. No calls. No texts. Could she have overestimated how much she meant to him? He'd never even called her his girlfriend. They had no label, but he meant... everything. Everything to her. The thought that he might be hurt, suffering, and she'd never even know—God. Susan choked back a sob.

No crying. It was time for action. She'd go to the fucking hospital and wait there until someone told her what the hell was going on, since no one else seemed willing to give her any information.

Keys in hand, Susan shoved her cell phone into her pocket and ran out the front door, not bothering to turn off the TV or even lock up. No one locked the doors way out here in the boondocks anyway.

The smell of smoke affronted her nostrils, and she looked up in surprise at just how much the ashes falling seemed to resemble snow. They landed in her hair, blew onto her eyelashes, and she blinked back tears from the irritation. *Oh, fuck, Trent. Please be okay.*

"Those better not be tears for me, baby," a low, strong voice said.

"Oh my God." She couldn't believe it. She hadn't even heard Trent's pickup truck pull into her gravel driveway.

He strode toward her on the grass, still wearing his uniform, still covered in soot and ash. When he dropped his long fireman's jacket onto the grass, his muscles bulged from the past twenty-four miserable hours of fighting the forest fire.

"You sure are a sight for sore eyes, Susie," he murmured, wrapping her in a bear hug, crushing her body against his. He was soaking wet with sweat and filthy with soot. The smell of the fire clung to his uniform, but none of that mattered.

"You asshole," she sobbed, forgiving him even as she said it. "You scared me to death. I was on my way to the hospital to check on you."

"I texted you as soon as I got off. I had to see you."

"But I never got a text..." *Damn phone.* "Never mind. It doesn't matter. All that matters is you're okay."

He brushed some ash out of her hair, a crooked smile on his handsome face. His teeth looked blindingly white compared to his sooty face. "I'm not used to seeing you with snow in your hair. It looks good on you."

"I'm not used to seeing you so...dirty."

"Does it look good on me?" Trent reached up and pulled down his suspenders, one by one, then tore off his sweaty T-shirt—revealing a tan, muscular torso beaded with sweat.

Susan could only nod mutely. *Yes. God, yes.*

Trent looked to his left and right, as if to remind himself they were truly alone out in her corner of the county. No neighbors in sight.

Without a word Trent lifted her up over his shoulder, smacking her ass hard. She dropped her car keys in the grass and laughed, exhilarated to be in his arms once more.

"I need to fuck you, baby," he growled. "So we either do it here on the grass, in the smoke and ash, or we go inside and get your nice clean bed all dirty."

Her pussy clenched at his words. "Fuck me here, Trent. Now." Outside, she felt animalistic and...ready. So fucking ready. He could get her wet with just one of his smoldering looks.

Trent set her down slowly, letting her body slide over the front of his as he released her from his fireman's carry. Her ass still tingled from the smack he'd given her.

"Do you spank all the women you rescue when you throw them over your shoulder?" she asked, feigning jealousy.

"Nope." He leaned in, his stubble scratching her cheek. "But I always want to."

Susan giggled and grabbed the suspenders hanging down his hips on either side of his uniform. "You don't need these to keep your pants on right now, you know that, right?"

Trent grinned and sat down in the grass, looking up into the smoky night sky just as she had done not moments before. "You want me to get buck naked right here?"

"More than anything."

Trent pulled off his boots, tossing them to the side. Susie watched with anticipation, running her tongue over her lower lip.

"This ain't no show, baby," he teased. "Take off your shirt for me."

Susan pulled it up over her head so quickly she heard a seam rip. Fuck it. She couldn't get out of her clothes and onto her man fast enough, as far as she was concerned. All those hours worrying, wondering... She kicked off her shoes and shimmied out of her jeans.

Trent stared at her as he pulled his pants off, the reflective stripes gleaming in the dark. He looked tall and dark and almost menacing in a sexy-as-hell way, naked, sweaty and streaked with soot. The look in his eyes made her feel desirable. Needed.

God knows she needed him, too.

"I was so scared, Trent," she admitted.

"Yeah, me too," he admitted, as he pulled her into his arms, his sweat-slicked chest rubbing against her breasts.

Her nipples immediately hardened into tight buds. "You were scared?" The thought never occurred to her, somehow, that a man as big and strong and courageous as Trent could ever be scared of anything.

"Yeah. Scared I was never going to get the chance to see you again." He lifted her up, and her thighs spread to lock around his waist.

She was dripping wet and so ready for him, but his revelation, combined with her arousal, made her gasp with surprise when his hard length impaled her.

"You feel so fucking good, baby," he murmured, sliding her body up and down his cock as if her weight was nothing to him. Carrying around that heavy fire hose all night, it probably wasn't anything he couldn't handle.

She threw back her head and moaned with pleasure, letting him control her body, their rhythm. Every thrust hit a tender spot deep inside her that made her want to stay wrapped around his body, standing and fucking in the front yard, forever.

With a moan she melted into him, her orgasm coming over her in slow waves that left her gasping for breath.

"That's my girl. I'm laying you down now," he whispered. "Don't worry. I gotcha."

Worrying about anything, once she was in his arms, would never happen. It was when he was gone, walking into a fire everyone else was fleeing from, that she worried.

He kept himself inside her as he laid her on the prickly grass, covering her with his muscular torso. Ashes from the sky fluttered around her face, and she buried her head in his neck to protect her eyes and nose. He smelled like the fire, like the woods.

"Hold tight," he growled, and her cries of ecstasy were

muffled against his neck as he rammed into her in hard, long strokes that quickened as he grew closer to his own climax. With a groan of satisfaction, he pulled out, a hot jet of his come covering her belly.

She smiled up at him, blinking away the white ash that covered her lashes. "Why were you scared you'd never get to see me again?" she asked, cuddling against his naked, dirty torso, letting the sticky come on her belly slide between their bodies. She wondered vaguely if they should hose off before entering her house for a proper shower.

"Don't matter now that I'm here with you."

"I think it matters."

"I was scared, Susie. What can I say? Some of my squad got hurt. Trees were burning, falling, the smoke was so thick I could barely breathe even with my mask on..." He paused and shook his head as if to clear it of the memory. "And then all I could think about was how much I wanted to get back into your arms."

Susan nodded, rubbing her face against his chest. "Why? Why me?" *Please, please tell me. Make it real.*

"You're gonna make me say it, ain't you?"

"Yeah."

Trent laughed and sat up, looking down into her eyes. "'Cause I love you. You know that."

"Now I do," she whispered, then laughed giddily in return. "And I love you too."

"Well, all right then." He picked her up, naked, and tossed her over his shoulder. "Let's go get clean so we can get dirty again."

He walked back toward her front door, leaving their clothes and his uniform in a pile on the lawn.

"Hey, what about our clothes? Your boots?"

"Leave 'em for later," he said, smacking her ass to punctuate his words.

Susan squealed, loving every second of it. Loving him.

"Now you know the truth 'bout how I feel," he said, "I get to do whatever I want to this ass, ain't that right?" His voice was filled with mischievous glee.

"How about you take my ass to the shower?" she suggested, staring at the rippling muscles of his back from her upside-down position.

Trent laughed. "Will do." His voice quieted. "I'm so fucking glad I got a second chance to tell you."

"Me too." Her eyes teared up.

I love you, Trent.

FIRE
EXTINGUISHER

Rowan Elizabeth

Middle-of-the-night sirens wake me. I pull up on my elbows and my covers slip down past my breasts.

Fuck. I hate midnight runs.

I tune in on the direction of the sirens. If they get louder, the guys are headed for downtown. If they grow dim, it could be the interstate. I can't wish for either. No one wants a house fire. No one wants a nasty wreck.

The sirens scream closer and then past, one street over.

"Be careful, guys," I whisper into the dark and flop back into my pillow. I desperately want to call my husband. But he's on that ride. Geared up. Adrenaline pumping. So, I pull the covers up to my chin and wait for his text when it's all done.

Eric has been on every type of run. The ones he laughs about and the ones he won't talk about, even to me. I hope tonight's run is another black-humor night.

But then I hear more sirens as the ambulance and a couple of police cars follow.

Eric's in charge of the fighters on this run. He's the shift lieutenant—always in control and fiercely tough. He never stands
back and barks orders. He's in the smoke and flames or in a
gasoline pool with the rest of them.

I am firmly on the awake side of sleep. He'll text. He always
does.

At six-twenty-three in the morning, he texts me a simple
message.

It was ugly.

He'll need me today in a way he doesn't always need me.

I get up and begin getting ready for him.

Eric will shower off the soot and smoke and stench from his
skin and come home to me in his blue work T-shirt and pants—
provided another run doesn't make itself known.

I down a Diet Coke and protein bar for energy as I make up
the bed. I reach behind the covers at the head and pull up the
soft rope ties. I take in a deep, humming breath as I run them
through my fingers. Too soft to make marks, unless one really
fights hard.

I pin up my hair and jump in the bath, where I shave everything smooth. I dry and lotion and slip into a tight, floor-length
blue nightgown.

I putter around, straightening the house a bit, until I know
his shift is over and I've heard no new sirens.

My heart beats faster when I hear the garage door open and
then close behind his SUV. He'll be exhausted, so I simply wait
in the kitchen for him to come through the door.

I watch as he pushes the door open and sees me. I smile and
open my hands, beckoning him.

I see his strong body relax in relief. I know what he needs.
After a night like this one, he no longer has to make every decision.

"Come here," I tell him.

Eric slumps in on himself and reaches me in three long strides. Leaning in, he wraps his thick arms around my waist and rests his head on my breasts.

I let him relax into me as I stroke the skin of his shaved head. A shiver of anticipation runs through me. He feels the electricity.

I lift his face between my two hands and kiss his lips. "Follow me," I instruct him.

I take his hand and walk toward the stairs. Leading him up, I feel the tension in his grip. It was a bad night. Worse than I will imagine. It will make the paper. I will read about it. He may or may not talk to me about it. But for now, that doesn't matter.

We reach our bedroom and I bring him to the end of the bed.

"Sit down."

I kneel down and unlace his boots, removing them.

"Take off your shirt."

Eric pulls at his tee and rakes it up over his head. I take it from him and lay it on the laundry basket.

I run my hands over his muscled chest and push him down on the bed.

"Scoot up."

Eric inches up the bed and rests his head on the pillows.

"Shut your eyes."

I run my hand up his left pant leg as I walk around to the head of the bed. Over his taut belly and chest, I trace my way.

I reach for his arm and pull it up to the rope. Expertly wrapping his wrist in the soft bind, I tie his left arm to the bed. He doesn't flinch, but relaxes into it.

Half-tied would work for any other night. But not tonight.

I straddle his prone body and stretch his right arm up and

out. The rope encompasses his wrist nicely, and he's all mine—control relinquished. I smile.

"Whatever shall I do with you?"

Eric opens his eyes and smiles.

"As though it's up to you," I say before I lean in to kiss him.

I force my tongue into his mouth. Eric makes a delicious sound and I bite at his lips.

When he's like this I could devour him. I chew on his lips and down his neck to his broad chest. His nipples are too tempting not to bite.

Eric sucks in air as I press down harder than usual on his right nipple. Under my hips, I feel his cock twitch in anticipation. I grind down against him to elicit a moan. I'm not sure from which of us it comes.

I'm tempted to simply strip him naked and ride his hard cock. But he needs so much more than that. He needs to lose control entirely.

Sliding down his body, I fuss with his belt buckle and pants. I take longer than necessary, to antagonize Eric. He begins to squirm under my hands, and I calmly place my hand on his belly to hold him still. He obeys.

I don't like Eric to waste his energies fighting me. I want them saved up for an explosive come. He's earned it.

Once I have his pants undone, I pull them down his strong legs and leave them in a pile on the floor. My lack of patience has me pulling at my negligee, half-tearing it before it hits the floor.

I crawl up the bed, treating myself to skin on skin.

I reach Eric's cock and rub my cheek on its heated, smooth skin. I want him in my mouth, but I find the strength to move up and cradle his cock between my heavy breasts. I wrap him in my warm breasts and begin to stroke his hard length with them.

I could exist on the sounds coming from him—moans and sighs and intermittent pleas for carnal release.

"Not yet, baby," I tell him. "I'm going to come first. You can watch if you want."

I crawl up to nestle in the crook of his arm. It's the next best thing to being held by him while I get off. I root up against him and moan at the heat of his chest pressed against my side.

I run my hands up my belly to my breasts and massage them painfully. I groan into Eric's arm.

I look to him and he's watching me with half-lidded eyes. They make me want to untie him and let him have at me. But that's not in the plans.

I squeeze my nipples and then press three fingers into Eric's mouth to gather his saliva.

"I'm getting off now."

I split my pussy lips with my fingers and rub Eric's spit into my cunt. The fire that jumps from clit to brain is outstanding.

I grind against my fingers and Eric's side. He rubs his foot up my shin and the meager contact makes me jump.

I arch and wriggle until the raging orgasm comes to the surface.

I cry out with the first.

He will bring the next.

Gathering strength in my legs and facing his feet, I straddle Eric's face.

"Make me come again," I tell him.

Eric's mouth makes contact with my cunt and I yelp. The second come rips through me just as my mouth reaches his cock.

Hard and hot, Eric's cock fills my mouth. He starts to buck under me, trying to get stronger purchase on my pussy with his mouth, trying to get his cock deeper in my throat.

I pop up on all fours and growl. "No."

Eric settles quickly into the bed. Only the tension in his feet betrays his false calm.

I flip around to his side and, holding his hips, take his cock in my mouth. He fills me perfectly to the point of gagging. But I'm controlling this show.

His salty pre-come slicks the back of my mouth and I circle his cock with my tongue.

I work his beautiful cock with my lips and mouth until I know he's ready. So ready. But this will not be the end for him.

Popping him out of my mouth, I lean back on my hand and begin rubbing myself. I get so very close to coming, but save it for the very next moment.

In a swift motion, I stand Eric's cock up and slide down on it. Impaled and filled.

This is when my Eric wants to fight the tethers. He's told me he wants to grab me by the waist with his strong hands and force me down on him, fucking the living hell out of me. But he doesn't get that today. Today, I will fuck him.

I move slowly and deliberately, taunting him with the idea of the pounding he really wants. Balanced on my thighs, I rise and fall on his cock—relishing the feel of him penetrating me.

The muscles of Eric's arms tense and flex against the ropes. His hands pull at the tiny length of rope left to him. He thinks he wants to be free.

He is wrong.

He wants to let go and I will not stop until I have sucked the control from him.

"I'm going to come on your cock, darling," I tell him.

I reach between my legs and feel the erect flesh inside me. It sends a thrill through me, and I take our fluids to rub into my clit. I buck and thrash on his body as I pull another come out of me.

It's time to take his.

I slide off my perfect perch and slip between his spread legs. His cock is straining against his belly and jumps when I wrap my hand around it. He's so slick with my come, I can easily slide my hand along his length.

I put two fingers in my mouth and suck them slick. Pressing them to his anus, I push in as the stroking of his cock accelerates. Eric's unearthly moans are my encouragement.

I pump his ass and cock simultaneously, knowing he will come soon. He will come and he will come hard.

For a moment, I'm tempted to take it all from him and make him wait through another orgasm of mine. But I desperately want to see the come ejaculate from his hardened cock.

I lean in and suck on his testicles and that does it.

Eric arches, his ass clamps down on my fingers, and his cock spurts out its contents all over his belly and chest.

Eric breathes hard with an occasional moan.

I slide my fingers from his ass and stroke his thigh as I sit up.

Admiring my handiwork and the art of his ejaculate on his torso, I relax. I crawl up the bed and tuck in against Eric's heaving chest.

We rest like this until Eric's breathing is under control. I reach for the tethers to release him.

In the morning light of our room, I hear, "Not yet. Please."

It was an ugly night.

HER HERO

Catherine Paulssen

With a soft swish, the papers blew off the wall and swooshed back again. Holly looked up from the fresh Batman sheets she was putting on her son's bed. Above the nightstand, Patrick had pinned newspaper articles and photographs of his dad and his unit. Engine 29 of the Eighth Battalion. Holly let her eyes wander over the cutouts.

Captain Nathan Keenan and Men of Engine 29 Awarded Medal of Valor

Mayor: First Responders' Actions Nothing Short of Heroic
Firemen's Ball Raises $25,000

A picture of Nathan and the men from his company—Tommy, Michael, Dion...their closest friends. So close, in fact, that each one of them was playing a role in raising Patrick.

A painting Patrick had made of his father in front of a burning building, holding a hose, fighting the flames.

A picture of all of them on St. Patrick's Day: Tommy and his wife Linda; their neighbors, the O'Connells; Nathan's parents,

Michael and Dion, with their families. Nathan was hugging her from behind. Both of their faces held happy, proud smiles. It seemed long ago that they had been that carefree.

Then a photo of the day when Nathan had brought old Mrs. O'Connell's cat down from a big oak tree in front of the neighbor's house—as well as her grandson, who had gone up after Mitzi and then, just like the cat, didn't dare to climb down again.

And the biggest photo of them all: Patrick wearing his dad's helmet, Nathan standing next to him, his arm around Patrick. How they looked alike—Patrick a tiny version of his father, flax-haired, freckled, his blue eyes blinking into the camera from underneath the helmet's rim. She had taken that picture the day Nathan made captain, two years ago. They had celebrated the promotion with a big barbecue. Their friends had all told her how proud she must be, all the women how lucky she was. It had made her glow with pride to know how much the men admired Nathan and how much the women envied her. And how could they not? He was a dedicated firefighter, he had a beefcake-calendar body, and he was a doting father.

Was he a good husband, too?

Holly straightened the blanket. Yes, yes he was. Every marriage went through tough times, she kept telling herself. And lately, they had hit theirs. However, she wasn't going to let a few arguments and an intense workload get the better of their marriage. Tonight, for their eighth anniversary, she would surprise Nathan with a three-course dinner and whatever he wanted to do afterwards. Patrick was spending the night at his grandparents' house, there would be champagne, and she had a new dress that made her feel like they were going on their first date again.

* * *

A few hours later, Holly sat in front of a cold asparagus risotto and melting crème brûlée. She watched the candles burn for a while. Drops of condensation ran down the bottle of champagne. Eventually she got up and started to clear the table. On her way to the kitchen, she caught a look of herself in the mirror. The dress looked foolish now.

She was about to go upstairs to change when the front door opened. Halfway up the stairs, she turned.

Nathan gave her a once-over. "You look beautiful."

She shrugged.

He frowned, then his expression changed. "Today's the nineteenth!" He dropped his keys on the table and walked over to her. "I'm so sorry. I tried to call but—"

"I put the phone on silent mode."

"Look, there was an emergency at the firehouse, one of the rookies—"

She raised her hand. "There's always something."

He turned his eyes away.

"If you had taken that administrative job at the Commissioner's off—"

"Holly, we discussed this."

"No, *you* decided it wasn't for you."

"Because it isn't!" He snorted. "I'm not one to sit behind a desk from nine to five."

"You would've had more time for us. You'd be home in the evenings and on weekends."

"You knew who I was before we married. I didn't change." She didn't answer, and his voice was adamant when he added, "Don't ask me to give up the job I love."

"When did it become more important than us?"

"It's not!" He took a step toward her, but stopped.

She could see she had hurt him, but she wasn't willing to propitiate.

"You used to be proud of me."

"I am," she said.

He threw her a look.

"I am!"

He shook his head, then turned around, grabbing his keys. Holly winced when the door fell into the latch. She heard the car turn on and leave. She sat down on the stairs and cried.

When the hurt and anger had numbed a little, she walked upstairs and let herself fall into bed. She snuggled underneath the blanket and buried her face in his pillow, in his scent, and drifted away...

That's when she heard his footsteps on the stairs, heard him entering the room. She felt his weight on the bed.

He pulled the sheets away and caressed her ankle. "I'm sorry," he whispered.

She sat up. "I'm sorry too."

His hand wandered up to the pit of her knee, and slowly, lovingly, he circled her skin with this thumb.

She pulled him close to her and pressed a kiss on his mouth. "Love me," she said.

He undressed her except for her panties and laid her down. It had always been a turn-on for her to be naked in his arms while he was still dressed. She watched him watching her and rubbed her thigh against his denim pants. Nathan's gaze wandered over the thin lace of her panties, then over her tummy to her breasts. He began to circle her navel with his fingers, tracing a line up her body. When he brushed her nipple with the sleeve of his woolen sweater, she shuddered. Satisfied with the reaction he evoked, he brushed her nipple again.

She made a little noise and he slid two of his fingers into

her mouth. She obediently sucked at them and sighed when he pulled them away to swirl them on her nipple.

He pressed his fingertips against her lips once more and watched her run her tongue over them, then continued playing with her nipples, teasing her until she arched her back and squirmed.

Nathan leaned in, and when the prickly fabric of his sweater rubbed against her tender, hard tips, she purred. "Nate...fuck me now."

He simply smirked. "Not yet, baby."

Holly moaned as he buried his face between her legs and rubbed his nose against the wet spot on the crotch of her panties. He hooked one finger into her panties and tugged them down a bit. She closed her eyes when he kissed the patch of skin above her delta. He traced her hairline with kisses while caressing the insides of her thighs, then slipped off her panties.

Instead of caressing her pussy, he started drawing lazy circles around her breasts. He prodded her lips with his and kissed her again. She groaned as her nipples were licked, sucked, rubbed, kissed, flicked by his tongue and pinched between his fingers until they were dark and swollen.

She wriggled underneath him and nestled against his sweater. "Undress," she breathed, and watched him taking off his clothes. Her finger ran over the scar where he had been injured on a rescue operation. She traced the hollow where his neck met his chest and the muscles of his arms, and kissed every inch of his skin from his hips to his armpit up to his neck.

She gasped when he rubbed her clit with his fingertip. His eyes held hers. She kissed him and wrapped her legs around his waist.

He stroked her flushed cheek. "I love you." He eased his body into hers and thrusted until every fiber of her was humming and

her mind was a blur. Nathan clutched the sheets between his fist
and, with a long groan, sank down on her.

She placed a kiss on his shoulder, feeling warm and soft and
heavy. With a content sigh on her lips, she snuggled her head
against his chest. She heard him mumbling her name in the
darkness. He continued to whisper words she had been longing
to hear, and his voice carried her away as she drifted back into
dreams.

Holly woke in an empty bed the next morning, her new dress
still next to her. Her heart thudded. She'd only dreamed. She
stretched and ran her fingers over the silken fabric. A little smile
spread over her face...

It should have been their weekend. Just the two of them. She
couldn't let yet another fight get in the way of all she had imagined it to be. Or what she had dreamed it would be last night.

Certain Nathan had spent the night at the firehouse, she
jumped into her car.

She drove into a bend. Sunlight blinked in the window of
another car, flashing into her eyes, and the moment she realized
the car in front was stopped, it was too late.

With screeching brakes, Holly crashed into the last of several
cars bumped into each other ahead of her. The impact flung her
forward; her car spun around and came to a halt. She felt the
pressure of the airbag against her face, taking her breath away,
before her body was hurled against the door as another car hit
hers.

For a few moments, the world around her turned black. She
thought of Patrick—and Nathan. And like those pictures and
cutouts on the wall in Patrick's room, her own memories passed
by her inner eye.

As the airbags that had cushioned both impacts deflated, she
opened her eyes. It took her a moment to realize she was alive,

but trapped between cars. Her head spun and dust particles from the airbags irritated her eyes, but she didn't feel injured.

She could hear sirens approaching. At the crash's other end she saw firefighters jumping out their trucks. She glanced around. A woman sat slumped over the wheel of the car that had collided with hers; her eyes were closed and blood trickled from her forehead. Police cars approached up from behind the bend. The passenger's side of her car was smashed. Her only way out would be through the trunk.

She struggled out of the belt and climbed into the back of the car. While searching for a tool to open the dented door, she noticed smoke. Heat. Flames reflected in the car's side-view mirror.

"Holly!"

She heard her name being called, and as she turned her head, Nathan appeared next to her car. Tommy and Dion were right behind him. They started to cut open the car that had crushed into hers.

"Come back to the front," Nathan yelled over the noise of the machines, the wailing of the sirens and the screams of people around them. He made a gesture to the car's back, and that's when she saw it. Surges of smoke billowed over the rear of the car. Sweat ran drown her neck, and the smoldering heat clawed around her throat.

"The flames haven't reached the inside of the car," Nathan said.

His words did nothing to calm her down. Her gaze darted across the car's floor, searching for signs of fire.

"Holly!" he yelled through the glass again. "I'll get you out. Okay?"

She answered, but not a sound came out of her mouth.

He smiled briefly, took off his coat, and, through the smashed driver's seat window, handed it to her. "Put this on."

She slipped into the protective gear, and Nathan climbed on the car's demolished hood.

"Get down," he shouted, and she did, hiding her head between her arms. She heard the blow of something heavy against the windshield, the splintering of glass, and curled up as tight as she could as thousands of shards rained down on her.

"Don't move," she heard her husband's voice, and again the shattering of glass. "Keep your eyes closed." Underneath her feet, she felt the heat intensifying, burning her feet through the soles of her shoes. More slivers hit the dashboard, and then two strong hands grabbed her shoulders. She didn't dare to open her eyes as Nathan pulled her up and out of the smashed vehicle. He pressed her against him and carried her away from the crash, away from the flames that now crackled in the trunk of her car.

She looked up at him. His face was blackened with soot. He was sweaty. He was hers. She kissed him and took off his coat to put back on him.

"Are you okay?" he asked.

"Yes." She snuggled closer against him. "Yes, I'm okay now."

He wrapped his arms around her and gently rocked her in his embrace. "Go over to EMS, baby. I'll be with you soon."

She nodded. "Nathan!" she called out to him as he was about to walk away.

He turned. His eyes scanned her face, then he smiled and winked at her. "I'll be careful."

When the crashed cars were nothing more than black shells and nothing more remained of the fire than a film of dirt, foam, and wreckage on the street, Nathan met her at her ambulance.

"Are you hurt?"

She shook her head. "What about you?"

"Just some scratches." He took off his helmet and jacket and sat down next to her. "When I saw your car in the middle of those crashed cars..." He cupped her face. "For the first time, I felt what you must feel each time I go on a tour."

She nestled her cheek into his hand. His skin, still heated, smelled of rubber, smoke, and sweat. "Did the woman in the car behind me survive?"

"Yes. No casualties. One driver's in critical condition, though."

"You saved my life. You couldn't have done that from behind a desk."

"Then somebody else would have rescued you."

"But you did." She kissed his fingers. "I dreamed of you last night."

"You did? What kind of dream?"

A little smile flashed over her face. "Are you...tired?"

He gave her a calculating look.

She blushed a little and averted her eyes.

Nathan took her hand, pulled it to his chest, and waited for her to look at him again. "I'm not," he said quietly.

She played with his fingers. "When I drove here, I was thinking of that night when we had just started dating—you were late because of an operation and I waited for you at the firehouse..."

A smile spread over Nathan's face. "And you ended up wearing my jacket and boots?" He tucked a strand of hair behind her ears. "And nothing else, just that black bra and panties underneath..."

She smiled back and nodded. "You made love to me in the backseat of my old Ford Pinto."

"The Pinto! God bless that car." He laughed. "You were

so hot that night," he added with a mischievous sparkle in his eyes.

"I'm wearing a black bra right now."

He winked. "And I've got the jacket..."

Holly laughed and he kissed her. "Let's go home."

JOHNNY BLAZE

Delilah Devlin

I held my iPhone in front of me as far as my arm could reach and took a picture, then quickly sent it to my Facebook page. *Yes! I don't know how Syl managed to talk me into it, but I'm at HardCox!!! Happy birthday, me!*

I posted the photo, then slipped my phone back into my purse, which I'd placed beneath the small round table where Sylvia, Heather, and I sat next to the raised stage.

"You took a picture of yourself?" Sylvia giggled and held out her hand. "Give me that phone!"

"No way, you'll just post pictures of the dancers' asses."

"And their *hoses!*"

My eyes bugged. "My mama would be horrified!"

I was already beyond mortified at being here—a male strip club, of all places. Syl didn't have to add kerosene to the fire burning in my cheeks. But she'd had me at one name: "Johnny Blaze."

So I had a thing for firefighters. Or, at least, one in partic-ular—who didn't even know I existed. The picture on the sandwich board outside the club—of a fireman wearing suspenders attached to the hose covering his privates—had been the deciding factor after I'd dug my heels into the concrete side-walk. His body reminded me of my secret crush. Syl knew all about my private infatuation. She'd pointed to the board, then, while my jaw slackened, whipped me through the entrance.

Now she laughed and lifted her Mai Tai, eyes shining with devilment. "See anyone you'd like to take home?"

I eyed the dancer currently on the stage now—"Davey Crockett"—who wore a coonskin hat and a striped, bushy tail covering his parts while he did the helicopter, much to the delight of the audience whooping and hollering all around us.

"Nope," I said tightlipped. My own gaze followed that twirling tail, hypnotized. It had been forever since I'd seen a cock. To see one with a bushy tail was just bizarre. I raised my voice to be heard over the loud rock music. "How long do we have to stay?"

Syl shook her head and raised a finger in the air to hail a beer-bitch with a tray of Jell-O shots. A blue cup landed on the table in front of me. Rather than fight Syl, I raised the drink and threw it back, gagging a little before gulping it down.

Alcohol never sat right with me. It made me hot. Something I didn't need now, because my cheeks were already a fiery beet-red. Alcohol, added to the tanned, waxed, buff bodies gyrating so close that splatters of sweat already spotted my blouse, left me feeling completely out of my element. The only reason I was still sitting here was because I had to see Johnny Blaze—not that any stripper would match up to the man of my fantasies.

Davey Crockett raised his arms over his head and did a flip, landing near the edge of the stage, his beaver tail slapping his belly, then his thighs.

I couldn't help where my gaze landed—I wondered how much

was furry sock and how much was his pleasure stick. Lord, the man was probably gay, anyway. I slid the napkin from under my drink and fanned my face.

The music stopped. A handsome man dressed in dark slacks and a black leather vest walked to the center of the stage. "Evenin', ladies," he said into the microphone he held, his thick Texas drawl sweet as syrup.

The crowd shouted back, "Evenin', Jason."

The women knew the announcer by name? Good lord, they needed to get a life.

Then he snagged my attention: "We have a birthday girl in the audience!" The audience erupted in laughter and catcalls.

My eyes rounded. I shot a look at Syl. "*Nooo....*"

Syl smiled slyly back. "You're only twenty-five once, cupcake."

Two nearly nude men swished through the curtain at the back of the stage, one a bald white dude wearing a biker's bandana and leather chaps. The other was a black man with a chest a bodybuilder would cry over.

Jason cupped a hand over her eyes and scanned the audience. "Where can she be?"

Syl and Heather bounced in their seats, arms flying, hands pointing toward me.

I hunched low, wondering if I could crawl beneath the table. The two burly men were coming straight for me.

"Syl, I'm going to kill you," I hissed.

Her smile was so broad I didn't know how her face didn't split in half. "You are going to thank me, baby girl. Just you wait."

When both men flanked me, I stubbornly kept my gaze lowered, pretending I didn't see them. But the black guy gripped my elbow and gently brought me to my feet. Then they both formed a chair with their arms and pushed the "seat" beneath me, nudging me hard enough to collapse my knees. As they swept me up, I gripped their arms, sure they'd drop me as they climbed the stairs to the stage.

I'm not a little girl. At five-foot-eight and nearly 180 pounds, I gave them a workout—not that they seemed to strain. A *wooden* chair had been brought to the center of the stage. They stood me in front of it, then the biker pressed me into it with a hand on my shoulder.

Knowing I was going to have to go with it or look like a complete coward, I flopped into the chair and folded my arms across my chest.

Jason produced two large white squares and raised them over his head. The crowd began to chant. "*Hoo-hoo-hoo!*"

Not until he handed them to the biker and both men went on their knees did I understand. "Uh...why do I need knee pads?"

The biker flashed a brilliant smile. "To save your pretty knobs, sweetheart."

My eyebrows crept up. I wanted to ask why, but I suspected his answer would send me dashing off the stage.

Biker boy slipped off my pump and smoothed a pad up my calf, fitting it to my knee. His buddy did the same, thankfully not at the same time or I'd have wound up flashing my crotch.

I was having serious misgivings about my outfit now—a shortish black skirt that had seemed flirty but demure when I'd dressed at home and a black, short-sleeved button-down blouse. With large silver hoops and a thick silver cuff, I looked "cute but casual," or so Syl had said when she'd scoured my closet for just the right outfit. Since our destination had been a secret until we pulled into parking lot, I hadn't given her choice of wardrobe another thought.

Now I wished I'd worn jeans, something to cover the length of white leg the men were still fondling. Biker dude stood, lifted me to my feet with a firm hand at my elbow, then marched me to the edge of the stage.

With Syl and Heather grinning like idiots, I knew he wasn't just sending me back to my chair. Behind me, the curtain whooshed again. The crowd drove to their feet, whistles and shouts rising so loud I wanted to cover my ears. I didn't dare look back.

"John-*nee*! John-*nee*! John-*nee*!"

My heart stuttered then burst into a wild tattoo. Heat burned my cheeks—but also began to pool between my legs. Funny how a little thing like a man with a hose can turn a girl's insides all weepy.

Biker dude gripped my shoulders and forced me to turn.

Johnny Blaze stood, framed by the curtain, his fireman's hat tipped low in front, the stage lights gleaming on the shiny top and shadowing his features. His tanned chest and ripped abs were bare except for red suspenders—thankfully, attached to yellow turnout pants. His large feet were encased by black boots. He raised a finger and curled it—twice.

I shook my head, glancing behind me to find the stairs, but gentle pressure on my shoulders forced me to my knees.

"Gotta crawl, Bridget," biker dude drawled. "All the way on your knees."

He knew my name? Kneeling, I cut him a quick glance. "I'm in a skirt."

His smile gleamed white against his darkly tanned face. "I know. Sweet how that worked out."

And because I knew I'd been set up and that I couldn't back away from the challenge now, I bent, pulled my skirt down in the back to cover my ass, and started to crawl on hands and knees toward the fireman who stood stock still, his hands fisted on his hips.

Lord, he looked so much like my inappropriate crush that what had been a trickle became a warm gush against my panties. I imagined it was him, that he had me in my bedroom, crawling toward him and his lovely baggy pants. The things I'd do...

Only the closer I drew, the deeper my suspicions grew.

His chest rose and fell too quickly—not something I'd expect from a guy who hadn't yet danced his way around the stage. His expression was hidden, but the angle of his jaw, so rigid, so still, reminded me of the new fireman in my hometown I'd been lusting after for weeks.

The reception desk at the library faced the front door, which had wide glass panels looking onto the main street and the fire station on the other side. I'd spent weeks leaning on an elbow and sighing over the new guy, the one Syl said was single and not a player. She'd been trying to hook me up for weeks, inviting me to drop by with cookies for the men—something I'd done in the past, but which I'd refrained from doing since *his* arrival because I didn't want to seem too eager or desperate.

Besides, what would someone who looked like that want with me?

I kept crawling, but suddenly, two thick thighs gripped my waist. Biker dude straddled my waist, but kept his weight from me. With one hand gripping my shoulder, he gave my ass a slap. "Don't stop now," he said loudly, slapping me lightly as I crawled faster, his body hopping to keep pace with me. The problem was, his thighs dragged at my skirt, and soon I felt cool air brushing against my bottom. I tried to reach back, but he was in the way. "My skirt!"

"Don't worry about it, sugar! Gotta have those birthday spanks."

My face got hotter; I started to sweat. I crawled, tugging his thighs along with me until I was three feet from Johnny Blaze, who had yet to move.

Biker dude stepped away. I pulled my skirt back over my ass, one cheek burning. A chair appeared beside me. Johnny moved, sat with his legs spread, and patted his muscled thigh.

The gesture was deliberate. I shook my head and glanced up again, seeing his face for the first time. My jaw dropped.

With a flourish, he tossed his hat away, grabbed my upper arm, and hauled me over his lap, face down.

Pushing up, I tried to lean away, but he stuck his elbow in my back, and I collapsed, the undersides of my breasts riding the side of one huge thigh. "What are doing here?" I whispered harshly.

"Giving you your birthday present," he drawled.

"Did Syl put you up to this?"

"Syl knows some things about me. Said you'd be into this. Are you?"

I craned my head around to look him in the eyes.

His dark brown gaze was narrowed.

"Not the way I saw our first date," I muttered, my voice going all breathy because I couldn't seem to catch it.

"I can't think of a better way to get to know you..." He flipped up my skirt.

I shrieked and reached wildly behind me, but my skirt was up my back. When his fingers dragged down my panties, I bucked. "Oh my freaking God!"

My big white ass was there for all the world to see. For Cooper James to see. I melted over his thigh, my breaths shuddering out and tears welling in my eyes.

A hand cupped the hot side. "Nice, Brady."

"You're welcome, man," biker dude said, chuckling beside them.

"So how many licks does the little lady get?" came Jason's voice over the loudspeaker.

"Twenty-five," shouted Syl and Heather.

"No, no, no." I twisted again to glare at Coop. "I already got a dozen from the biker."

His mouth curved. "Not by me, sweetheart. *Count.*" His hand raised.

I jerked my head forward, body tensing.

The first slap burned like fire.

"Ow?" I wriggled, to no avail. "That hurt."

"Good. You've been avoidin' me for weeks."

"I wasn't avoiding you," I whispered. "But I would have if I'd known you were a sadist!"

"Not a sadist, sweetheart, but I do like to make my woman hot." He slapped me again. "Count."

"Three!"

The strokes landed one after the other on the cheek Brady hadn't been able to reach as he'd ridden me across the stage. My ass burned. But so did my pussy, blood filling my labia, moisture seeped from inside me. "They're going to see!" I hissed.

"See what, darlin'?" His hand paused, lying on my bottom, but giving me a squeeze.

"That I'm we—"

He swatted me again, but this time at the center of my seam, fingers lingering, trailing in the wetness. His thighs bunched beneath my torso, then widened. Something hard bulged against my soft belly.

"Fifteen," I squealed.

"Yeah, let's finish this up," he said, his voice gruff now.

Swats landed on both cheeks, then against the backs of my thighs. I lost count and repeated a number, but he didn't seem to mind I was mathematically challenged. His chuckle made me wetter.

I skipped. "Twenty-five!" I screamed.

Laughter fell all around us. Fingers pulled up my panties, pushed down my skirt to cover my bottom. Biker dude grabbed my hand and dragged me up to stand beside him, an arm around my waist. He must have sensed my knees were weak, because right when I started to crumple, he held me against his side, turning me to the audience.

The women were laughing, clapping, but I didn't care. I glanced behind me at Johnny Blaze, no, *Cooper James*, who pushed off his chair. My tongue thickened. Was that drool pooling in my mouth? Lord, he was a beautiful man—all hard angles and thick muscles with dark, short-cropped hair and wicked eyes.

Brady leaned toward my ear. "You gonna fall on your ass if I let you go?"

I snorted. "If I do, it's padded."

His smile flashed. "Padded just right. You ask Coop. You didn't see his face, but he 'bout died when he bared it."

I swallowed hard, forced a smile, and gave a small bow to the crowd. I took a step, but a hand gripped my forearm and swung me. Before I knew it, my ass was in the air again, my body bent over a broad shoulder. Glancing down, I didn't need to see the yellow pants to know whose hard ass had me.

The walk through the curtains and down the hallway behind it was brisk. "Is there a fire?" I asked, bouncing on his hard shoulder.

"Yeah, in my pants."

I barked a hoarse laugh. "You can put me down now."

"We're not there yet."

The loud crash of the emergency door opening at the end of the corridor was the first indicator that Coop had something besides finishing my birthday-girl spanks on his mind. He strode into the parking lot.

I pushed against the sexy small of his back and tried to look around him. He was heading for a shiny red pickup. His. I knew because I'd watched him peel out of the station's parking lot often enough.

A door slammed open and he dumped me on the edge of the seat, then tucked my legs inside. "Get your belt on."

Had to admit, the gruff texture of his voice as he barked orders turned me on. I reached for the belt and buckled in, watching as he walked quickly around the front of the truck and climbed into the cab beside me.

With his head and chest bare, suspenders covering his nipples, I could barely draw a deep breath. And I needed it. My mind was whirling, my body humming with excitement. "Syl tell you to show me a good time? Does she pimp you out to all the girls?"

"You have a smart mouth," he said, starting the ignition and putting the truck in reverse. The tires screamed as he pulled quickly out of the lot and hooked a left toward the highway and our own small town. "Makes me think of all the ways I want to stuff it."

My jaw sagged. "That how you talk to your girlfriends? No wonder you're single."

"No, just to you. I'm going to be very clear. Don't want to start this thing without you understanding a few things first."

I crossed my arms over my chest and lifted my chin. "Like?"

His glance darted from the road to me. "Like, I want your

bare cheeks on my leather seat."

My expression must have been every bit as outraged as I felt.

His mouth twitched, then flattened. "Now, Bridget. Ass on leather. Now."

So you have to be wondering why I didn't just tell him to fuck himself. I wanted to. But as soon as I thought the words, I knew I wanted the arrogant jerk to fuck me. Hard. Every way I'd always imagined.

He knew I was hot. I knew he was hard. There was no mistaking what tented his pants. And I wanted all that stuffed inside me. Right then. I eased up and slipped off my panties, then pulled my skirt up in the back where it bunched. My ass sat on the cool seat, and my excitement leaked onto the leather.

"Pull it up in front," he said. "I want to see your pussy."

No protest from me there. I wanted him to see it, too. I pulled up my skirt, tucking it under the belt to keep it high, then went a step farther and opened my legs.

Leaning back, I gripped the belt above my shoulder and held very still, wondering what he'd do next, not believing that I was sitting beside my fireman, my lower half completely exposed. My breasts tingled, the tips pushing against my lacy bra. My pussy clenched.

His lack of reaction had my breath leaving in a slow disappointed drain.

But then the truck veered off the road.

I screamed and grabbed for the dashboard.He pulled quickly onto a gravel road, drove another thirty feet, then slammed the brakes.

My body jerked forward and back. Before I'd righted myself, he was out the door and stomping around the front. My door slammed open, his hands released the buckle then turned my body to face him, spreading my legs.

Just when I wondered if he was a serial killer who'd found just the right spot to bury me, he climbed onto the truck rail and leaned inside. His hands clutched the back of my head and his mouth met mine in a fierce, blistering kiss.

I dug my fingers into his hot shoulders and held on. He rocked into me, his bare chest gliding against my clothing, and it wasn't enough. I pulled back. "Please."

His eyes closed. He drew a deep breath then leaned his forehead against mine. "Back at my house," he whispered harshly, "I have the AC cranked low enough we can start a fire in the hearth. I have candles ready to be lit. Wine on the hearth with two glasses. Birthday cake in the fridge. I'll give you roses, make it sweet...like you deserve." His eyes opened, his gaze boring into mine. "But right now, Bridget, I need your hot pussy on my dick."

I gasped, then gave a sharp laugh. "I don't think a man has ever said anything that crass to me before."

"Sorry, but I'm so hard right now, I can't think."

I smiled. "Didn't say I didn't like it..."

His head tilted. A grin stretched. "Scoot that butt off my leather. You're gettin' it wet."

I ducked my head and flirted from beneath my eyelashes. "Sorry, didn't mean to make a mess."

"Yes, you did," he said tapping my nose. "But I won't spank you again—if you do what I say. Scootch."

I edged closer.

His hands reached around me and cupped my buttocks. He stepped down, bringing me with him.

I snaked my arms around his shoulders. "I'm too heavy for this," I said, thankful for the moonlight so he couldn't see my mortified blush.

"Baby, I can handle you. Don't worry."

"I'm not little."

"No, you're not. But I like your curves, I like your soft ass. I can't wait to fuck it, make you howl—but that'll come another time."

My mouth dropped open, and I shook my head. "Again, no man's ever been that rude to me."

"Honest, baby. I'll always give you that. I like your fleshy body. Like the way you bounce, all over, when you walk. It's my thing. Syl knows. I've been hot for you since the first day I saw you walkin' up the library steps. Knew I had to have that ass."

Caught between dismay and a strange, shuddering joy, I readjusted my grip on his shoulders. "Hurt your back and I won't be happy."

"Afraid you'll put me out of action?"

Laughing, I lifted my chin. "You want this ass? Well, I want something of yours too."

He jostled me, gripping my bottom hard, as he ground his cock against my spread lips. "Am I lucky enough you want this?"

I gave him a narrowed glance. "I have to warn you. I read."

His eyelids dipped, his smile broadening. "Got some fantasies I can help you with?"

"A few." *Okay, a lot.* But that was for later, too. Once I knew him well enough, and once he wasn't looking right at me when I told him. "We have a problem," I said, walking my fingers across one sturdy shoulder.

"Do we?"

"You forgot something."

"I have condoms in the glove box, but Syl told me you're on the pill. I'm clean, sweetheart. Clean bill from my new-hire physical. She can show you."

Nice having a friend who works for the town's HR. "Not the problem I was talking about, but good to know."

"Then what? Got a boyfriend I need to help you lose?"

"You know I don't. I'm not exactly every man's dream girl."

"Baby, you're *my* wet dream." When I gave him a doubtful glare, he tsked. "I won't ever lie. I want you, Bridget Luckadoo. Fact, is I like everything I know about you, everything I've seen. I've waited so long for a chance at you, I'm barely civilized."

I rolled my eyes. "You still have your pants on."

"You know what to do. I'll just lean you against the truck..."

He did. I pushed his suspenders off one shoulder, then the other. He bent his chest to brace me and leaned his hips away as I clumsily shoved down his pants.

Lord, he hadn't been wearing anything under them all that time. "What the hell? If you'd danced..."

"I had no intention of dancing for anyone but you."

Now that his important bits were naked, I wasn't in such a hurry. "What were you doing on that stage anyway?"

"Used to strip when I was going to school. I was young. It was easy money." He shrugged. "I still have friends. They helped me set this up."

"You went to a lot of trouble."

"I wanted to make an impression."

I waggled my eyebrows. "You did."

He gripped my bottom, fingers digging into my still-warm skin. I gave a gasp, but smiled to let him know I liked it.

"The shirt—your bra, too—lose 'em." I hastily followed his orders, and then gasped when air trailed over my tightly budded nipples.

"No comin' 'til I say so," he growled, his gaze flickering over my naked chest.

Instead of sliding me down his dick, he stepped up again

and laid me on the leather seat. My back slid on the wet spot I'd made. His hands pushed my thighs up and over his shoulders, then smoothed up the insides, stroking my knees, my soft inner thighs, halting right beneath my shaved pussy.

His thumbs opened me, and he bent and blew a stream of air across my wet flesh.

I clenched, my cunt making a lewdly juicy sound.

Coop growled and ducked his head. His mouth closed over my swollen lips and sucked, tongue darting out to skim between my folds. When he flicked my clit I gasped and bucked, my fingers digging into his thick hair.

He shook his head and I eased my grip. He leaned back, his dark gaze glittering. "Now, these are the spanks I really wanted to give you." He raised a hand and slapped my open cunt.

The impact shocked and thrilled me. His large hand covered my entire sex. His fingers slammed my cloaked clit. Again and again he slapped, the sounds sharper, the sting growing hotter. My sex swelled. My gasps became weak, mewling cries, and my bottom bounced on the leather as he drove me closer and closer to completion.

When he dragged his wet palm away, his nostrils were flared, his jaw tight and sharp enough to cut. He wiped his fingertips on my nipples, then with a groan leaned over me to draw one into his mouth.

There was nothing gentle about the way he gobbled me up. He was so eager, so rough, I nearly came from his strong, suctioning pulls.

He gave me a nip, then backed away, chest billowing as though he'd run a race.

My glance roamed his heaving, sweat-slicked chest, his taut muscled abs, then dropped to his cock.

His glance dropped, and his smile was crooked as he gave

himself one long stroke. His erection was massive—thick and long, the head blunt and fat.

"Turn. Bend over the seat."

My glance flew up to lock with his. There wasn't an ounce of mercy in his taut face. Beyond worrying whether he'd like the view, I did as he commanded, clumsy in my eagerness to obey. His hands guided me until I stood on the rail, my ass out the door but my torso draped on the seat.

Hands gripped my bottom, parted my cheeks.

I held my breath. When the thick, bulbous head butted against my pussy, I groaned and opened my stance, inviting him deeper.

He popped my ass with a sharp slap, then drove deep, burrowing his big cock inside.

Swollen, hot, and drenched, my pussy clenched around him, already rippling with the first vibrations of a cosmic orgasm.

"Not 'til I say so," he whispered behind me.

I shook my head and groaned. "Can't stop it."

"You'll learn."

Lord, when he said things like that—as if we'd do this again, as if he meant to teach me something, about him, about me, I really couldn't help it.

Liquid gushed, coating his thick shaft, and he began to move, his motions strong and rhythmic. He pulled my hips and my back dipped, giving him a better angle to slam into me. His strokes quickened, sharpened, until our bodies slapped together, making lush wet sounds that added to the other noises we made...grunting, groaning, my excited mewls growing more shrill, until I broke.

I keened, pushing up as he powered into me, building a scalding friction that prolonged my orgasm, my breaths chopped apart by his jackhammer thrusts.

His muffled shout followed. Scalding spurts bathed my channel and trickled down to wet my mound. His strokes slowed until he rocked gently against me, as though he didn't want the pleasure to end.

When he pulled free, I slumped against the seat. But he didn't let me linger there. Again, his strong hands moved me, turning me to face him. He pushed his still-hard cock back inside, then raised me up and slid me off the seat and into his arms.

He stood in the moonlight, hugging me close, our bodies still connected, not a single sign of strain tightening his features. "Told you I could handle you," he said, his voice gruff again. "You okay?"

I grinned and leaned toward him, wrapping my arms around his shoulders and my legs around his trim hips. "Best birthday ever."

"And we still have that fire to burn." His smile was warm and wide. "Wonder how we'll top it next year..."

But I read. I have a few ideas.

ABOUT THE AUTHORS

CYNTHIA D'ALBA started writing on a challenge from her husband and discovered having imaginary sex with lots of hunky men was fun. Her first book, *Texas Two Step*, was released in 2012 and became a publisher bestseller.

ADELE DUBOIS is happiest when driving her convertible with the top down. She is a multi-published, award-winning author of erotic romance novels, novellas, and short stories. When not at the beach, Adele and her Navy-hero husband enjoy their eastern Pennsylvania home, where she is working on her next novel.

SHOSHANNA EVERS is a critically acclaimed, bestselling romance author. She is published with Simon & Schuster/Gallery, Ellora's Cave, and Penguin/Berkley Heat (Agony/Ecstasy), and her work is in several Cleis Press anthologies (including *Best Bondage Erotica 2012* and *2013*). She lives in Los Angeles with her family and two big dogs.

ROWAN ELIZABETH has enjoyed sharing her naughty ideas for almost eight years. Published with Susie Bright, Cleis Press, Naughty Nights Press, and MuseItUp Publishing, Rowan has been having a great deal of fun.

RACHEL FIRASEK normally pens paranormal romances, but couldn't miss the chance to play with a smokin' hot fireman.

CATHRYN FOX, realizing the corporate life wasn't for her and needing an outlet for her creative energy, turned in her calculator and briefcase and began writing erotic romance full time. Cathryn writes paranormal and contemporary stories from her home office in Eastern Canada.

ILY GOYANES is a writer, editor, publisher, and miscreant. Her work has appeared in several anthologies, including *Best Lesbian Erotica 2012,* and she is the editor of *Power Plays* (Ampersand Editions) and *Girls Who Score: Hot Lesbian Erotica* (Cleis Press).

NANETTE GUADIANO is a writer whose poetry has appeared in numerous literary publications. Her prose and fiction have appeared in publications including *Fifteen Candles* (HarperCollins, 2007) and *You Don't Have a Clue* (Arte Publico Press, 2010). She loves Italy and firemen; her story is a tribute to both.

TAHIRA IQBAL has been writing since she can remember. Her work went from thrillers to romances, until she realized she could merge the two. Drama, danger, and sex in good, measured doses is what she writes best.

ELLE JAMES, at home in Northwest Arkansas, is busy writing tales of murder and suspense for Harlequin Intrigue. Her first Harlequin, *Beneath the Texas Moon,* was released in March 2006 and was a Romantic Times Top Pick! She's since written numerous intrigues, and is now writing for Harlequin Nocturne.

M. MARIE lives in the heart of downtown Toronto, Canada. This passionate young Canadian is soft-spoken, inquisitive, and addicted to art, writing, and videogames. She is also too embarrassed to ever admit how much of her story is based on a real experience—and a real cat.

CATHERINE PAULSSEN's stories have appeared in *Best Lesbian Romance 2012* and *Girl Fever,* in Silver Publishing's *Dreaming of a White Christmas* series, and in anthologies by Ravenous Romance and Constable & Robinson.

LYNN TOWNSEND is a geek, a mother, a dreamer, and the proud owner of a small black hole residing under her desk that tends to eat kittens, odd socks, staplers, and her car keys. Her work has been published with Cleis, Torquere, and PriveCo.

KALISSA WAYNE has always been a writer. Since the tender age of twelve she has written stories that spoke to her heart. She is still following that dream. Kalissa lives in southern Louisiana with her husband of thirteen years, BB, and struggles with being a Yankee living in Cajun country.

MAGGIE WELLS, by day, is buried in spreadsheets. At night, she pens tales of people tangling up the sheets. She'll tell you she's a deep-down dirty girl, but you only have to scratch the surface of this mild-mannered married lady to find a naughty streak a mile wide.

SABRINA YORK, Her Royal Hotness, writes naked erotic fiction for fans who like it hot, hard, and balls-to-the-wall, and erotic romance and fantasy for readers who prefer a slow burn to passion. An award-winning author in multiple genres, Sabrina loves writing all kinds of hot, humorous stories.

ABOUT
THE EDITOR

DELILAH DEVLIN is a prolific and award-winning author of erotica and erotic romance with a rapidly expanding reputation for writing deliciously edgy stories with complex characters. Whether creating dark, erotically charged paranormal worlds or richly descriptive historical and contemporary stories that ring with authenticity, Delilah Devlin "pens in uncharted territory that will leave the readers breathless and hungering for more" (*Paranormal Reviews*).

Ms. Devlin has published more than one hundred twenty erotic stories in multiple genres and lengths. She is published by Atria/Strebor, Avon, Berkley, Black Lace, Cleis Press, Ellora's Cave, Harlequin Spice, HarperCollins: Mischief, Kensington, Montlake Romance, Running Press, and Samhain Publishing. Her published print titles include *Into the Darkness*, *Seduced by Darkness*, *Darkness Burning*, *Darkness Captured*, *Down in Texas*, *Texas Men*, *Ravished by a Viking*, *Enslaved by a Viking*, *Shattered Souls*, and *Lost Souls*. She has appeared in

Cleis Press's *Lesbian Cowboys*, *Girl Crush*, *Fairy Tale Lust*, *Lesbian Lust*, *Passion*, *Lesbian Cops*, *Dream Lover*, *Carnal Machines*, *Best Erotic Romance (2012)*, *Suite Encounters*, *Girl Fever*, *Girls Who Score* and *Duty and Desire*. For Cleis Press, she edited 2011's *Girls Who Bite* and 2012's *She Shifters* and *Cowboy Lust*.